BLURB

How the hell did I, the perpetual bachelor, end up accidentally married in Vegas—to my client?

As soon as I find out who's trying to kill her, we'll get a quickie divorce...or will we? I was never supposed to be married. I was never supposed to fall in love. I was never supposed to put her in danger.

But now that she's back in my life I wonder if some things shouldn't stay in Vegas.

To keep her I'll have to fight for her. Good thing I'm brazen enough to do just that.

*The conclusion to the Brazen duet

STILL BRAZEN

M. MALONE

NANA MALONE

Still Brazen © February 2019 M. Malone and Nana Malone

MALONE SQUARED

This book is a work of fiction. The names, characters, places, and incidents are products of the writer's imagination or have been used fictitiously and are not to be construed as real. Any resemblance to persons, living or dead, actual events, locales or organizations is entirely coincidental. All rights reserved. No part of this book may be reproduced, scanned, or distributed in any manner whatsoever without written permission from the publisher except in the case of brief quotation embodied in critical articles and reviews. For information address: MALONE SQUARED, 340 S Lemon Ave #9016, Walnut , CA 91789

ISBN: 978-1-946961-27-3

STILL BRAZEN

CHAPTER ONE

Hailey

"God, you were always treated like a goddamn princess."

What was he talking about? Yeah, Dad and I had a great relationship, but Mom never loved me. But I knew better than to say that to him.

"Look, we all love you. And I'm just – honestly, I'm just trying to survive. I'm just trying to do the best that I can for this company, Mom, Dad, you. I never meant to shut you out."

"God, you've got everything. Dad bent over backward to make you feel loved and wanted."

Where was he going with this? Was he upset that Mom was drinking again? Or is this about what I'd just seen?

"Evan, I don't know what you're talking about. I love you. I don't know why you hate me. You never used to. I was always the one that you would come to. You used to talk to me. And it just changed."

"I didn't change. This is me. The perpetual disappointment."

"And six months ago, what the hell did I do to you? You started acting like—" I didn't finish that. I was going to say that he'd, started acting like Mom. "You started acting like you didn't care. Like you hated me. Like I'd done something to you, and I still can't figure out what I did to deserve your loathing. You stopped coming to work. You started gambling."

His brows snapped down. "You don't know what you're talking about."

"Yes, I do. Who do you think paid your debt two months ago at the horse races? You made a bet out there and Deborah Lachlan approached me. I was kind of embarrassed. So I just—I made it go away."

"I don't need you to do anything for me."

"You're my brother."

"Stop saying that."

"Why would I stop saying that?"

He ran his hands through his hair, tugging it. All I could do was stare at the gun.

"Evan, just put the gun down. We'll talk about this, okay? You don't have to do this. Whatever you think you need to do, you don't. You and I can fix everything."

He lifted his brows then and shook his head flatly. Then he glanced down at the gun. "This? This is for protection. There's someone out there shooting." He exhaled a long breath. "And yeah, okay fine, I've been gambling a little. And there are some people that want money that I don't necessarily have right now, so I got it for protection."

"Okay, I get it. But maybe you could put it down now."

He lifted his gaze to peer at me and shook his head. "You think I would hurt you?"

"What am I supposed to think?" To be safe, I began to back away because he still held the gun, and I wasn't sure if the safety was on. "Evan, in case it has escaped your notice, there's a maniac out there shooting people."

"What? And you thought it was me?"

"Well, yeah. You came into the safe room with a gun."

"This is the safe room, remember? I'm part of the inner circle. I knew that this was a safe room."

Had he? I couldn't ascertain the truth of that. "Okay, then tell me what the hell is going on. What happened six months ago?"

He tugged at his hair again. "Fuck! Why can't our parents just fix their own goddamn problem?"

"I have no idea. Why don't you tell me what's happening?"

"It's all about you. As always."

"Explain, because clearly, I don't know what the fuck is going on."

He chuckled then. "Ah, there she is, the real Hailey. The one you never let out because, God forbid, you'd look less than perfect."

"Fuck you." I knew I shouldn't have said that, but goddamn it, I was tired.

He laughed then. "You know, I actually prefer it when you're you. At least you're honest."

"I am honest."

"Whatever. You just need to be perfect."

"I try really hard to be perfect for Mom. We'll just—" I didn't finish. I wasn't going to give him that piece of ammo.

"Isn't it enough that you have Dad?"

"I don't think it's unreasonable to want both of my parents to love me."

"When I found out, it was like everyone had fucking lied to me."

"Found out what?"

"God, you don't even know? How dumb are you? You're adopted! I found out six months ago. And considering that you've worked with Dad to edge me out of my own company, I assumed you knew."

Just hearing the words come out of his mouth let the

wind out of my sails. I didn't even care if he shot me at that point. I eased into one of the conference chairs and let the air seep out of my lungs.

So it was true, the images I'd seen. The dates had been right.

"Fuck, you really didn't know?"

I shook my head. "No. I didn't know."

My brother frowned then. "So, Dad giving you a piece of the company, all this time, you didn't do it on purpose?"

I shook my head. "Evan, I would never do that to you. I would never force you out. This is your home as much as mine. I had no idea. I didn't try to steal the company from you, or whatever the hell it is that you think I've been doing. I wanted Miriam to be a success so Mom would be proud of me. So that she would—" I took a deep breath. "So that Mom would love me. Pathetic, I know. Saying it out loud, I recognize how sad it sounds."

Evan eased into the chair across from me and laid the gun on the table. "You really didn't know?"

"Nope. I just saw the pictures from the presentation, and I thought they had the dates wrong because, if they were right, Mom should have been huge. But she looked basically the same. I thought it was a mistake. I—I didn't even imagine something like this."

Evan's body sagged as he slouched into the chair. "Well, fuck!"

Oskar

"What the fuck do you mean he got away?"

Matthias's voice came over the coms. "Everyone has reported back. No shooter."

"Okay, where is she?"

Rafe's voice was clear. "I'm out back with Tyse having another look around. Hailey is in conference room one."

I took off running. I just had to see for myself that she was okay. I called her, but she didn't answer.

"Come on. Come on. Come on." I called her again. Straight to voice mail. "I'm heading for Hailey."

Everyone confirmed on the coms. The sooner I could get out of here, the better I'd feel. We were missing something. Whoever this asshole was, he was three steps ahead of us. I ran down to the board room. When I opened the door, there was a flurry of activity. Hailey was at the conference table, and so was Evan, but he was standing with a gun in his hand. I had my weapon out in one second. I tapped my com unit. "May day, conference room." That was all I needed to say. Everyone would come.

Hailey stood.

"Oskar, wait."

"Wait for what? He has a gun on you."

Evan threw up his hands. "Oh, for fuck's sake."

I steadied my gun on him. "Stop moving, asshole. I happen to be a crack shot." Evan, the asshole, did not drop his weapon. The side door opened and Rafe came through, gun raised, but he didn't fire.

I shifted my glance to him for a second. "What the fuck? Shoot."

Rafe assessed the situation and shook his head.

"Asshole. Hailey, baby come here. Are you okay?"

"I'm fine. He's not going to hurt me. Evan, tell them you're not going to hurt me."

"I have zero intention of hurting my sister."

"Great, asshole, then drop your fucking weapon." I kept my weapon raised and shifted my body in front of Hailey's. She tried to shove me out of the way, but yeah, good luck with that. I softened my voice. "Hailey, are you okay?"

Her voice was softer too. "Yes, I'm fine. Are you okay?"

I scoffed. "Yeah, clearly. Except, my girlfriend's brother is trying to give me a fucking heart attack."

I could almost hear her smile. "I'm your girlfriend?"

"Actually, technically you're my wife."

"I do like how you say that."

I rolled my eyes. "Rafe, what the fuck?"

Rafe shook his head. "You know the directive. You don't shoot unless there is clear and present danger. Right now, he's not aiming the weapon. But dumbass should fucking let it go."

Evan shook his head. "What guarantee do I have that you guys aren't going to shoot me unarmed?"

Hailey tried to peek out from under my arm. "I will guarantee it. Gentlemen, do not shoot my brother."

Rafe didn't budge. He didn't even glance her way. I, on the other hand, just tucked her back behind me. I was wearing a bullet proof vest. But in her dress, low cut as it was with a slit so close to heaven I wouldn't even have to take the damn thing off to fuck her, she was not bulletproof.

Evan shook his head. "You have to put your guns down, and I'll put mine down."

I shook my head. "That's not how it works, asshole. You have a gun on your sister, I keep my weapon. And you really don't want him to shoot you. He likes killing things. I don't relish the thought. It would piss your sister off."

Evan swallowed hard. He shifted his gaze to Rafe and then back to me. Slowly, he eased the gun onto the table. At that moment, Tyse and Jonas came running to the door. Matthias was fast on their heels.

Noah was in my ear on the coms. "What the fuck is happening?"

I spoke evenly. "Evan Livingston thought it might be fun to hold a gun on his sister. And your boy Rafe, Sir Kills-a-lot, isn't shooting him."

Rafe eased forward, making sure that Evan didn't reach for his gun again. Then quickly, he secured him.

Tyse, apparently knew his job, because he came over with the zip ties and had Evan's hands locked and loaded, and was already taking him from Rafe.

Rafe grabbed the gun and stuck it in his back. I glowered at him. "Oh sure, now you want to think before you shoot people."

Rafe just shook his head. "I didn't even shoot at you. You think you'd let that shit go."

"Never."

I pulled Hailey out from behind me, and I ran my hands over her face. Her neck, her shoulder, her breasts. Hey, I just had to check that the girls were okay. And then finally, her torso and her back. She was uninjured as far as I could tell. "I just had to see for myself."

She raised a brow. "You needed to test my tits to see if they'd been shot?"

I nodded sagely. "You never know. Sometimes adrenaline can make you not feel any pain, so I had to double check."

She shook her head. "What is going to happen to my brother?"

I pulled her close and kissed her forehead. "Let's get home. We'll deal with it after that, okay? I just want you safe and out of here."

"It's not what you think." She pulled back. "I swear. He wasn't going to hurt me."

God, I wished I could believe her. "We'll sort it out at the penthouse, okay? Come on. Right now, I just want to make sure you're safe."

For once, she didn't argue with me.

CHAPTER TWO

Hailey

They wouldn't tell me anything.

I fumed silently, watching as Oskar and various other members of the Blake Security team came and went, all of them tacitly avoiding my eyes. The most logical response to the events of the last few hours should be fear, but I was too far gone to even be scared. I'd blown past scared and straight to furious.

Evan had pulled a gun on me! Sure, he claimed he hadn't been planning to use it, but the more I thought about it, the less certain I was of his words. After all, he'd been lying for months about my true parentage. Who knew what else he was hiding?

Outside observers to our relationship might think I should have at least considered the possibility that Evan might want to hurt me, but I'd always thought our contentious relationship was like so many other sibling relationships. Competing for parental attention could make you unfriendly but not homicidal. How had I missed the signs? Or was Evan just that good at pretending?

I hugged my arms around my middle. Even if Evan didn't feel the same way, I would always think of him as my big brother. The boy who'd once pulled my pigtails, shared his candy with me and made the most epic blanket forts. Whether we shared the same bloodline or not, we would always have those memories.

It was going to take a while before I was ready to face this new world.

Oskar entered the room again. I jumped up and stepped in his path so he couldn't ignore me.

"What's going on? I want to know what's happening with my brother." When he wouldn't meet my eyes, I crossed my arms.

Oskar sighed. "He's being interrogated by Matthias."

Going through my mental catalog of all the guys I'd met recently, I shivered a little remembering the intense young man with the tattoos. He'd been friendly enough, but there was something in his eyes that made me sure he was anything but.

Just then the elevator doors opened and Priya walked out followed by Dylan.

"Hailey! There you are!" Priya rushed forward, arms open, and I accepted the hug gratefully.

All the emotion I'd been suppressing spilled over and I clung to her, burying my face in her shoulder. How had things gone so wrong so quickly? Just a few hours ago I was worried about whether I would nail my speech not whether my only sibling was trying to kill me.

"Are you okay? What happened? They wouldn't tell me anything." After sending a sour look over her shoulder at Dylan, Priya took my arm gently and led me over to the couch in the waiting area.

"I think... I still can't believe this, but Evan might have been the shooter."

Her eyes rounded. "Oh no. I'm so sorry, Hailey. What the hell is going on with Evan?"

"I wish I knew. We've always fought but all siblings fight, right? But tonight, there was something different about him. He didn't look right." My lip trembled remembering the hatred in Evan's eyes as he'd raised the gun and pointed it right at me. "He really hates me, Priya. My own brother hates me."

"Oh sweetie." Priya pulled me into another hug, rubbing my arms gently. It was exactly the comfort I needed just then after having my entire world turned upside down.

"Is it stupid that I want to believe he's innocent? That maybe there's something else going on and he wasn't really trying to hurt me?"

"Of course, it's not stupid. He's your brother. You just want to believe the best. It's not your job to believe the worst. That's why you have us." Priya looked behind us to where Oskar and the others were standing in a group talking. "If you have to be in danger, this is a good team to have on your side."

Oskar broke away from the group and walked over. Priya looked between us and then squeezed my arm. "I'm just going to make you a cup of tea or something."

As soon as she left, Oskar sat next to me on the couch. He looked uncomfortable. Not that strange considering what had just happened, but it still made me nervous.

"What is it? Did you find out anything else about Evan? What about my parents? I know you told me earlier they were fine but—"

Oskar held up a hand to hold off all the questions. "They're safe. Everyone is safe, actually. Your brother isn't a very good shot."

My shoulders slumped. "So you're sure it was him?"

His eyes were sympathetic, although he probably thought I was an idiot for holding out hope there was some other villain in the wings to blame.

"We'll know more when Matthias is done with him. But there's no more damning evidence than literally being caught trying to shoot someone. Fuck." He ran his hands over his face roughly. "When I think about what could have happened... if Rafe had been any slower, you might not be here right now."

I was moved by the emotions moving over his face. Not caring who could see us, I launched myself into his lap and pressed my lips to his. Oskar threaded a hand through my hair, dislodging the carefully arranged bun I'd styled with such precision earlier. Neither of us cared where we were or who was watching. All that mattered was this passion that sparked whenever we touched and reminded us what it meant to be alive.

I'd almost died tonight. Facing death brought a certain amount of clarity. Spending my entire life worried about rules and order hadn't brought me the things that really mattered. Love. Trust. Safety.

Instead, the most chaotic relationship I'd ever had turned out to be the one thing that was holding me steady.

The sound of a throat clearing brought me back to reality. Oskar groaned. "Duty calls. I need to go."

"Wait. There's something I need to tell you. When I was looking through the slideshow for my presentation earlier, I noticed something weird about a few of the pictures. They were dated right before I was born but my mom wasn't pregnant."

Oskar looked wary. "Hailey, there are some things we need to talk about. But first, I have to ask, do you know who put those pictures in the slideshow?"

I thought about it. "I'm not sure. Whoever worked on this

in marketing must have asked my dad for the photos. But Oskar, about the photos. Evan said that I'm adopted."

Even though my stomach felt like it had dropped through a hole in the ground, I needed to say it aloud. Evan's words had been rolling around the back of my mind this whole time.

To my surprise, Oskar didn't look at all shocked. He took a deep breath. "We just recently found some medical records that indicate Miriam Livingston did not give birth to you. We were trying to confirm it before we said anything."

I put a hand to my chest where my heart was suddenly racing. Maybe a small part of me actually had been holding out hope that Evan was wrong because the look on Oskar's face hit me like a battering ram. It was true, I could tell by the carefully sympathetic look in his eyes. Looking at the pictures was one thing but hearing it spoken aloud made it real. Miriam may not have been the best mother, but I'd never doubted that she was mine. Now it felt like everything I thought I knew about myself was up in the air.

"Breathe, butterfly. That's it."

Oskar's gentle hand on the side of my face brought me

back to reality, and I sucked in a deep breath. The slightly woozy feeling receded, and his face came back into view.

"Sorry," I croaked. "Please finish. I need to know."

I could tell by the stiff set of his shoulders that he didn't want to. Knowing Oskar, he wanted to throw me over his shoulders and hide me away from the world. But if we were going to figure things out, it would take both of us. Despite all the new information coming to light, I still had a lifetime of experience dealing with all of the key players.

"We think Evan might have seen those medical records at some point, too. If he doesn't believe you're really siblings, then that's motive. He might be trying to get you out of the way so he can inherit everything.

It made logical sense. It hurt so much to admit, but now with the benefit of hindsight, I could see how several weird things Evan had said recently made perfect sense in light of recent revelations. What was it he'd said while holding that gun on me?

Funny you should mention us being family.

It had seemed so strange and out of context then, but

now I wondered if this was what he'd been talking about. But there were still so many unanswered questions. How would Evan have come across Mom's medical records? It wasn't like they were just lying around. I was pretty sure Blake Security had done some hacking to get those, and my brother certainly wasn't skilled enough to do that.

Unless he'd had help.

"I hear you and I admit it looks really bad. But promise me that you guys won't just assume it must be Evan and not look any further. All we have are a bunch of assumptions at this point. We need to give him the benefit of the doubt."

Oskar's hand tightened on my waist. "Oh, butterfly."

And I knew by the look on his face that there was more.

Oskar

Why did I have to be the one to tell her? Watching Hailey break down was dredging up emotions I'd thought long dead. She'd been stoic throughout, keeping her cool even after Rafe had brought her in. Most people would have been distraught after being held at gunpoint, but she'd kept it together.

Until she'd seen how it had affected me.

Hailey tried to project this perfect, collected, cold persona to the world, but she broke down at the first evidence that I was upset. My butterfly wasn't nearly the cold robot she wanted to believe she was. She was warmth and light and love all buried beneath a diamond exoskeleton.

Now I had to be the one to chip away at that exterior again. First I'd had to tell her that her mother might not even be her mother. Now I'd have to break the fucked-up news that her brother had plenty of other reasons to want to take her out. About thirteen million of them to be exact.

"I wanted to tell you earlier, but Noah thought it was best to keep it under wraps until we'd investigated further. Evan is in debt. A lot of debt. With the wrong people."

She blinked and then nodded. "It's bad, huh?"

"Yeah, baby. I'm sorry."

"It's not your fault. I just don't know how we got here. Why wouldn't he just ask Dad for the money? He knows the family would have paid it off."

"I'm guessing it was pride. Like a lot of gambling addicts, he probably thought he could take care of it himself without having to reveal how much trouble he was in."

She sniffled. "I'm sure that's what it was. He always seemed so angry that I'm close with Dad. He said it was hard living in my *perfect* shadow."

I tipped her chin toward me until she could no longer avoid my eyes. "This is not your fault, Hailey. Evan has a problem, and he needs help. But it's not something that you could have prevented."

"I guess we'll never know, will we?"

This wasn't getting us anywhere. A bath and then a good night of sleep was probably the best medicine for what ailed her right now. But I knew I was probably going to have a hard time convincing her of that.

"I think that's enough for now."

Hailey shook her head. "No. It's not enough. I need to understand what's going on."

"You've done all you can for tonight. I promise that we're going to do everything we can for your brother and investigate every lead. But my job is to take care of you. To protect you. And that's what I'm going to do."

She didn't look impressed. "Even if that's not what I want?"

It cut through me with all the precision of a knife. "Yes, even if it's not what you want. The types of people your brother is involved with are dangerous. They wouldn't think twice about using you to get to him. I won't let that happen."

"Fine. I guess you'd know more about this world than I would." Hailey stood and stalked toward the back, where our room was.

I followed, trying to pretend her words didn't bother me. It wasn't as if I needed the reminder that we were from two different worlds. Every single day, I thought about the fact that Hailey could do so much better than me.

Why was it so different hearing it from her lips?

Once we were behind closed doors, Hailey ignored me as she got ready for bed. I averted my eyes as she stripped off the formal gown, throwing it on the floor before climbing into bed. She turned to face the wall, and I could tell by the stiff set of her shoulders that she was fighting tears.

Feeling like absolute shit, I tore off my dress shirt and stepped out of the tuxedo pants. I'd lost the jacket somewhere in all the frenzy, not that I cared. When was the next time I'd need a penguin suit anyway? The only reason I'd ever need one would be to accompany Hailey to her events, and considering the way things had gone tonight, that wouldn't be happening anymore. Once it was confirmed that Evan was behind it all, I'd probably never see her again.

CHAPTER THREE

Oskar

My heart felt like cement as I pulled on a pair of sweatpants, leaving my chest bare. I sat down in the desk chair across the room.

After a few minutes, Hailey glanced over her shoulder. "You aren't coming to bed?"

I shrugged. "Figured you didn't want me to. Since I'm such a dirty low-life and all."

As soon as the words were out, I cursed under my breath. I hadn't intended to say that. Something about her brought all my emotions to the surface. My insecurities were impossible to hide when she looked at me with those vulnerable eyes.

Hailey pushed up on her arms and regarded me with incredulity. "Seriously? I never said anything like that."

"You didn't have to," I mumbled.

She threw the covers off and swung her legs over the side of the bed. I tensed at the flash of golden-brown skin.

What? I was angry, but I was still human.

"I never insulted you. That was just a statement of fact. You know this world, and I don't. Apparently, I don't know *anything*. I'm just the stupid girl who thought she had a regular, although flawed, family. But no, I'm the girl with the lying parents and the homicidal brother!"

But the time she was done, she was almost yelling, and her cheeks were flushed red with exertion. She crossed her arms with a little huff that I found utterly charming.

"You're beautiful, is what you are."

She hung her head. "Don't do that. It's not fair to be all sweet and stuff when I'm freaking out."

I laughed and then finally stepped forward to pull her

into my arms. It had been torture not to touch her when everything inside of me was crying out to comfort her.

"Promise you won't let go?" Her voice broke and cocooned her against my body. She practically climbed me like a tree as I pulled her into my lap. The way she trembled in my arms almost broke me.

Here I was, worried about my own shortcomings when Hailey had been dropped into the middle of a nightmare. Being shot at and scared for her life was bad enough, but she was also dealing with the bombshell news about her family and ancestry. What she needed right now was an anchor, someone to hold her steady when it felt like everything was falling apart.

If anyone had asked me what it meant to be married before that moment, I probably would have said some bullshit about a white dress and rings, but in an instant, the meaning crystallized and I understood why people still bothered with vows and promises of forever.

Because in the worst of times, when the chips were down and you had nothing left to hold on to, all you needed was one person that you could count on. It was humbling and terrifying, but with all my soul I wanted to be that person for Hailey.

"I know that everything seems crazy right now, but I've got you. Nothing is going to hurt you if I can help it."

She squeezed me tighter. "Don't let go, Oskar."

I shifted slightly so I could lift her up and reposition us on the bed. After some maneuvering, I got us curled up together under the covers. Hailey's hand came down to cover mine, intertwining our fingers.

A sense of peace stole over me. She suddenly turned to face me, so close that I could see the dried tear tracks on her cheeks and the brightness of the tears still in her eyes.

"I just want to forget, Oskar."

If I had any doubts about what she meant, her hand rested lightly on my stomach right above the band of my sweatpants. Then she said the one thing I couldn't ignore.

"Make love to me. Please"

Hailey

I could see the indecision in his face. Normally you'd need a crowbar to keep Oskar away from me, especially if I was wrapped around him in bed. But the events of tonight had shaken both of us to the core. Oskar was a protector through and through. The idea of me being in danger was no doubt messing with his mind.

But I needed to take the control back. I was so tired of everyone else steering my ship. After everything that happened, it was hard to know who to trust. My mother may not be my mother, my brother might be a killer, but Oskar was still as he'd always been, the one person I knew I could count on to make me feel safe. To make me feel sexy.

To make me feel loved.

"I love you," I whispered, the power of saying it aloud flowing through me.

He stiffened but then his arm slid under my back, spearing through my hair.

"Hailey."

It was just one word but the weight of it settled right in

the pit of my stomach. Even though it hurt a little that he hadn't said it back, I could hear his emotions in just that one little word. The way he said my name made me feel like I was precious and that was enough for now.

When he paused, I thought that he was going to deny me, but then his lips skated over the skin at my throat. I hummed in pleasure, allowing my head to fall back into the cradle of his palm. Right then, I let it all go, fully surrendering to the moment. With Oskar, I found something that I'd never had with anyone else. Complete and total safety and trust.

"You've had a rough night, baby. I should let you sleep."

My hand trailed down his bare chest and then settled on the bulge in his sweatpants.

"This doesn't feel like you want to let me sleep."

His lips curved against my neck. It tickled a little and I squeezed him gently, happy with the resultant groan.

"No, I'm not going to let you sleep. Didn't you get the memo? I'm not a good guy, and I've never claimed to be."

There was something behind that statement, something dark and forlorn that made my heart clench. But before I could even think, Oskar shifted slightly until I was under him, and all my thoughts melted like butter in a hot skillet. That's all it took with him, one shift of his hips, a whisper of breath against my ear, and I was jelly. I had no willpower around the man, and it should have appalled me but instead it made me ache.

"Take this off." Oskar's gruff voice registered one second before his hands were on the hem of my T-shirt, tugging at it.

With a laugh, I allowed him to raise it over my head, and before the shirt cleared the bed, his mouth was fastened to one of my breasts. All the stress and tension of the day disappeared as he tugged, licked and bit gently. My hands clutched at his shoulders and then ended up in his hair as I tried to keep up with the whirlwind of sensations. I took the opportunity to trace over the muscles that I always drooled over, digging my nails into his biceps as his mouth worked its way downward.

"Yes. Fuck yeah, get those nails in me."

I shivered, unexpectedly turned on by the gruff command. If you'd asked me before Oskar whether I was into dirty talk, I would have said no. But there was something about the way he said things in that deep voice. It made me want to be wild and uninhibited with him. Like no matter what dirty, sexy thing we did together, it would never be wrong.

"Oskar!"

I cried out when he finally reached his destination, his huge shoulders settling between my thighs. While his tongue lashed, I clapped a hand over my mouth to keep from alerting the entire building that he was currently feasting on me like a starving man. I was still holding my mouth when the first orgasm rolled through me. Oskar's fingers tightened around my thighs as I trembled, and he made satisfied groaning sounds, like I'd pleased him.

By the time I opened my eyes again, he was rolling a condom on and wearing a very confident smirk.

"You look happy with yourself," I remarked, the scratchy sound of my voice only making his grin bigger.

"The girl of my dreams is in my bed and just came screaming like a siren. Hell yeah, I'm happy with myself. And I'm about to get happier."

He lowered himself slowly, our eyes locked the whole time. Then he pushed in just a little, giving me time to adjust. My mouth fell open at the pressure, his size always an adjustment. Then I curled my legs around his waist, drawing him deeper. I could tell by the veins on his neck and face that it was taking some serious restraint for him to go slow.

And that wasn't what I wanted.

"Don't hold back, Oskar. I need this. I need you."

He closed his eyes at my words, a visible tremble of need traveling through him. "I don't want to hurt you."

"You won't. I might be a little sore, but I can handle it. Just make me feel. Make me forget."

I squeezed my internal muscles, pleased at the hoarse groan it wrung from his lips. When he opened his eyes, I knew I was going to get exactly what I'd asked for.

CHAPTER FOUR

Hailey

No lie, I was definitely sore.

Whose fault is that?

Oskar had definitely been trying to take it a lot slower. But I'd been pissed, and then, well, hot. But even though I was sore, it was totally worth it.

As I slid out of the bed, he reached for me. "Where are you going?"

"I need a shower. I have to go to work."

"Okay, we can shower together."

I begged off. "Oh my God, I'm sore."

His brows snapped down. "Damn it, you should have said something."

"Last night I was busy enjoying myself. I didn't think about the ramifications of your giant tree trunk."

He grinned and winked at me.

I rolled my eyes. "Yes, you have a big dick, but you know this. Shower, okay?"

He nodded. "Just a shower, I promise."

I laughed, even as I shook my head, because I knew he wouldn't be able to keep his hands off of me. Most likely, he was just going to wash his two favorite parts. Well, three favorite parts. I would have the cleanest tits, anus, and vagina on the planet, before he was done.

I wasn't wrong either. That quick shower I was supposed to take lasted 45 minutes. When we finally stepped out, we heard someone banging on the door. He grabbed a towel, only after I insisted, and jogged to open it. Whoever was on the other side told him, "You better come out here."

I wiped the steam off the mirror and called out. "What's going on?"

"I don't know. But I think I hear your Dad."

I sighed. "Oh Lord. Okay, you go ahead. I'm coming."

I got dressed in record time. I'd forgone makeup and just opted for lip gloss, and I put my hair in a messy bun. I was only planning on working a half day today anyway. Despite how things had turned out, I still wanted to go in and congratulate everyone on a great job on Miriam and then give them all the rest of the day off. Hell, the rest of the week.

When I opened our bedroom door, I heard shouting from the conference room.

In my bare feet, I jogged down the hall, past the kitchen, and then to the conference room. "Dad, what is happening?"

He spun around and glared at me. "Do you know what they're saying about your brother?"

Evan stood gazing out at the skyline, but his back was tense, his shoulders hunched.

"Dad, calm down."

"I will not calm down." My father slammed his hand on top of the table, and I jumped.

Oskar immediately stood and came over to step directly in front of me. I attempted to shove him out of the way, but much like last night, that didn't work.

"Oskar, move. He's my father! He's not going to hurt me."

The giant idiot just crossed his arms. "Well, your father needs to calm the fuck down."

Of course, that just pissed Dad off more. He pointed a finger. "I brought her to you to keep her safe. And now what? You're accusing her family of trying to hurt her?"

I slipped under Oskar's arm. "Dad, no one is accusing anyone of anything. But Evan did approach me with a gun yesterday."

It was as if I'd slapped him. He jerked back and shook his head. "What?" And then he turned to Evan. "Evan, tell them you didn't do it."

If possible, Evan's shoulders sagged even more. "I can't."

"What the hell do you mean you can't? Tell these people that you didn't try to hurt your sister."

My brother turned around slowly. "Well, that one I can say. I didn't try to hurt my sister. I wouldn't." He lifted his gaze to mine, and I could see the shame there. But I could also see the love. "I didn't try to hurt her, but I did have a gun."

As always, I tried to mediate. "Daddy, it's really just a misunderstanding. Evan had a gun. Blake Security was just doing their job." I turned to the guys. "Thank you all very much. Now I know your team is extremely well-trained, and very cool under pressure." I turned back to my father. "But someone did shoot at me yesterday, so I am concerned about that."

My father scowled. "But to accuse your *brother*."

"Dad, it's not like—"

Apparently, Oskar had had enough, because he gently tugged on my elbow, pulling me back to his side, and he angled his body so that he was between me and my father.

"Sir, I need you to cool down your tone. We did as instructed. We kept Hailey safe. Evan is alive only because she requested it."

My father liked that even less. "You people are fired."

I sighed. "You can't fire them Dad, they're doing their job. And as it turns out, someone is actually trying to kill me."

"Well, I will find somebody better."

I tried to move Oskar again, and that was a no-go this time, so I peeked around him. "Well, Dad, I override you, because Blake Security has done a great job. I've never felt safer."

My father scowled, but it was Evan's voice that cooled everything off. "Dad, do you have any idea what it's like to be the black sheep of this family? The fact that people would even think that I could try and hurt my sister isn't surprising. Yes, I had a gun for my own protection. Because as per usual, I was an idiot."

My father shook his head. "You've made some mistakes. It happens. You just need to get back on your feet."

"No, Dad. I have a real problem. I pissed away my whole fucking inheritance. Pissed it away. And I need a gun to protect myself. Come on, we can't pretend none of this is happening. Sooner or later, you have to see things for how they are, the whole truth, and see your part in it."

My father frowned then. "See what part?"

"Dad, when the hell were you going to tell Hailey she's adopted?"

Even with my father's darker skin, I could see the red flushing up his face. "What are you talking about?"

"Dad, stop. I know. Hailey knows. We both know. Obviously, Mom knows, so maybe this whole family can stop fucking lying."

I tried to scoot out from behind Oskar again, but he shifted right in front of me. "Hailey, stay put."

I slapped his back, and damn him, I swear to God, he chuckled.

Noah stood. "Mr. Livingston, I know emotions are high at the moment. We'll leave you and your family to talk this out."

Noah, Matthias, Jonas, and Rafe stood to leave. Dylan followed, standing outside the door.

As they filed out, Oskar didn't even look at them. I guess, it was unsaid that he wasn't going anywhere.

"Dad." I shoved at Oskar, and when he didn't move, I pinched his ass. That got him moving. He glared at me.

"Well, you wouldn't move." I moved out from around him. "Dad, why didn't you just tell me?"

My father sputtered. "You didn't—you didn't need to know."

Evan sighed and sank down to one of the seats. "Dad, we both know. So why don't you just tell us. I don't remember us adopting Hailey."

My father sighed then. He still glowered at Oskar, but I could tell that he was beaten and was finally going to tell me what the hell was going on.

"Evan, that's because you were too young. When you were three and a half, almost four, I guess, I had an affair. I wasn't proud of it, and it was a short-term fling. Then the woman found me and told me she was pregnant." His gaze met mine for only a brief second and then darted away. "She wanted money, lots of it. She wanted to make the whole thing go away and for me to pay for her silence. I couldn't do it. I couldn't let her keep you out of my life, so I offered to adopt you instead. Your mother, Miriam... I didn't know it then, but she'd already started drinking. I don't think it was as bad as it is now. But, I'd started to notice her being off. I think my actions just exacerbated it."

Tears welled in my eyes. "Where is my birth mother?"

He shook his head. "I honestly don't know. She took her $3 million check, and she ran. But I got you. It was all I cared about."

"So, what? You just covered it up?"

"Your mother and I, we made a decision that for the company, the shareholders, for all of us, it was best that she adopted you. We made you part of the family."

"Oh my God, so you lied? My whole life, you lied to me."

"Hailey—" He reached for me, but Oskar stepped between us again. His voice was kinder this time.

"Mr. Livingston, you've just dropped a very large bomb on Hailey's lap. And she's going to have to diffuse it. So maybe we can just give her some time."

I didn't even have to be looking at my father to tell he was crestfallen. It was in his voice. "Hailey. Please—"

I shook my head and wouldn't look at him. My gaze was on Evan instead. "Just go. I can't look at you right now."

I waited until my father's footsteps became more distant, and then I met Evan's gaze. "I'm sorry. You got caught up in this as much as I did."

Evan sighed. "Yeah, but you know what? I was fucked in the head long before I knew. At the end of the day, they probably overcompensated and gave me whatever the hell I wanted. And I took advantage, so it was really my own fault."

Oskar sighed. "Okay, let's get this sorted." He turned to the hall and called everyone back in. The guys piled in, and he met Noah's gaze. "I think Evan can go, but with a guard dog."

The others sat down, but Dylan stopped when Oskar held out a hand to block him. "It seems I'm on guard dog duty."

Oskar grinned at him. Dylan didn't even flinch. "Why is it that I always get stuck with guard dog duty?" he grumbled.

When Evan left, for his own protection, he left with Dylan.

The rest of Blake Security stayed in the conference room while Oskar took me back to our bedroom. "Sweetie, maybe you shouldn't go into the office today."

Instinct had me protesting. "I'm going."

"For what? You clearly had a long day yesterday.

Someone shot at you. I know you want to celebrate with your team, but you can Skype them, or whatever. It's safer for you here, and I think you probably want to avoid your Dad for a bit, right?"

He had a point there. "Okay, fine. I just need to find my laptop."

"I'll get it for you." Before he left, he kissed me on the forehead. "Anything you need, I'm here, okay? You aren't alone."

I just wished I could believe that.

* * *

Oskar

I walked Elijah Livingston out. His back was stiff and his shoulders bunched. The guy was still pissed. I got it. But still, Hailey's happiness depended on him, so he needed to stop being an asshole.

"We're going to keep looking, Mr. Livingston."

He turned on me and jabbed a finger on my chest. "You have to do more than look."

"We are. We're not going to let anything happen to her. *I'm* not going to let anything happen to her."

I hadn't said anything to Elijah about me and his daughter yet. We'd all agreed that it was probably the safest thing to not tell him about me and Hailey being married. Those kinds of details would get lost in translation and do nothing but cause pain.

"You have to do something. This is my baby girl. You don't know the lengths to which I've gone to protect her."

I sighed. "She knows. And we're doing what we can."

"I know how bad this looks, but Evan would never hurt her."

"And I'm inclined to believe you because Hailey believes him. But we do need to keep an eye on him."

"And we can't ignore the fact that someone is out to hurt my family."

"Getting at one of the kids is how they're likely to do it. Not to mention it seems that Evan can't seem to keep himself out of trouble, so we'll get two birds with one stone. Dylan and Tyse will stay on him and help keep him out of trouble."

"The real culprit is still out there."

At the elevator, Elijah rolled his shoulders and cracked his neck. I could sense his need to get the hell out of there. He was twitchy, fidgeting.

I made eye contact with Ryan, silently telegraphing that he was to stick with Elijah like glue until he was safely home.

Tyse was in the follow car. To make sure Elijah wasn't a target. Both of them knew, they were done with the older Livingston, they needed to go give Dylan a hand with Evan. The dude was his own worst enemy.

If Evan somehow slipped Dylan's net, Ryan would be on him, and he wouldn't even know. Two-man teams were standard with Blake Security, but Evan didn't know that, which suited us just fine for the time being.

"We have people on both of your children. Like I said, nothing is going to happen to them."

Elijah squared his shoulders. "It had better not. I'm paying you people a lot of money. I feel like she should be safe by now."

I clenched my jaw and glared at him. "She is safe."

"Keep it that way. She might not want to speak with me right now, but she's still my baby girl." He shook his head. "I should have told her the truth. All those years I had plenty of opportunities. I tried to tell her so many times, but I just couldn't."

"Look, I don't have any kids, so I have no idea how this feels. But knowing your daughter even a little, something tells me she'll come around. Just give her time and space, and she'll figure it out."

Elijah nodded his thanks. When they were gone, I turned to find Rafe leaning against the kitchen counter and giving me a shit-eating grin.

"Oh, so Papa Don't Preach over there doesn't know that not only are you boffing his daughter, but you're his new son in law?"

I glared at him. "Shut the fuck up."

Rafe grinned back. "No way. This is going to be awesome."

"It already is awesome. I married the prize."

Rafe shook his head. "Yeah, but you didn't know you were marrying the prize then. Hell, you didn't even know you were married until just a little bit ago."

I shrugged. "It doesn't matter, because I'm winning this game of awesome here."

He just chuckled and shook his head. "I've been waiting for your comeuppance and—man, I can't wait."

"You just keep talking shit. That's never going to happen." Only problem was I knew he was right. I knew a reckoning was coming, and it wasn't going to be pretty for any of us.

CHAPTER FIVE

Hailey

Priya belly flopped on to the massive couch. "God, I can't believe I have to fly back to California before this is cleared up."

"I know. I've gotten used to having you here. It's been really fun."

"Well, you just have to come to Cali next time. Um, don't bring your murderous stalker though, because you know, it's kind of a thing trying not to get your bestie killed."

I tossed a pillow at her.

She popped a piece of popcorn into her mouth and

ducked easily. "Still too soon for you? In all seriousness though, don't do that thing."

"What thing?'

"You know, the thing. Don't push away a man who loves you."

A flush crept up my face. I was convinced fire was leaking at my ears. "He doesn't love me."

"Oh my God, are you blind? The way that man looks at you, if that isn't love... Shoot, he's so madly in love with you he doesn't even know what to do with himself. It's why he goes all caveman, 'let me club you with my big stick.'" She added a little dance for emphasis.

I stifled a giggle. "I only pushed him away because he broke my heart once."

"Well then, let him put it back together. You closed your-self off too much."

"I do not."

"You do too. You're so afraid someone is not going to love you back. I could kill your mother for that."

I groaned and flopped back against the pillow. "Please, let's not talk about my mother."

Priya munched on another piece of popcorn. "What, something else happened with her?"

"Oh my God, how did I not tell you?"

"Tell me what?"

After this morning's debacle, I'd had three Skype calls. I rushed to lunch, and then I convinced Oskar to at least take me to my office to thank my team and give them the rest of the week off. Then I came back here, and team Blake Security had dinner together, so this was the first time I'd seen Pryia alone all day. "Yeah, I don't even know where to begin."

"Begin with the most scandalous part, of course."

"Well, that's easy. It turns out I'm adopted."

Priya sat up, upending her popcorn. "What the fuck?"

"Oh yeah. Good times. Evan sort of held me at gun point last night and then broke it to me that he found out six months ago that I was adopted. This morning, Dad admitted he'd had an affair, and when the woman came to him to extort money from him, he paid her and made her give me to him. Then my adoptive mother, the one who has had a drinking problem since I was old enough to remember, adopted me. So, I think that pretty much covers all the basics."

Priya shook her head. "Wait, go back to the part where Evan held a gun on you."

"It was a misunderstanding. He wasn't really holding a gun *on* me, but he did have a gun because he's in trouble with some bad people for gambling debts."

Priya groaned. "Oh my God, I missed so much at that gala. Stupid gun shots. All I knew was Tyce dragged me out of there like my hair was on fire. Then he handed me off and the next thing I knew, I was being locked up here at the lair. Unfortunately, being locked up here at the lair did not involve me being tied to a bed naked by Tyce, which I should file a complaint about, honestly."

I choked out a laugh. "Oh my God, he doesn't even know what he's in for."

"Oh, I think he does. The way he eye-fucks me all the time, I'm convince he likes creative bitches."

"What happened to the TA you were doing?"

Priya waved a hand. "Oh, he's just for exercise. Tyce looks like a man who knows what to do with a woman like me."

"Who knows? Maybe he does like crazy."

"Enough about my crazy. Back to your crazy. Okay, so all I knew was that you were safe, and Tyce told me as soon as he had confirmation that they were coming back with you. Then he told me to get some sleep because you were already down for the night."

I nodded. "I fell asleep in the car. Oskar carried me up."

"Jesus. So, you're fucking adopted?"

"Yeah because Dad had an affair, which is... whatever. But the great news is my birth mom, she's a real gem. She just took the money and ran. No "How are you, I hope you'll be safe and loved.' She just took her money and disappeared."

"Hey, you were safe and loved. You father adores you."

And I couldn't deny that, but he lied to me my whole life. "I know he loved me, but that's not the point. The point is he lied to me and he was trying to make up for one mother who just didn't want me and another who also really didn't want me but was forced to take me."

She winced. "And Evan knew?"

"Yeah, he found out about six months ago. I didn't even

want to ask how. But that's when shit started to get worse with him. Yeah, he'd been sort of a wastrel before, but the gambling, the extra-hard partying, the women, the just general, overall not-giving-a-fuck, got really intense then. He thought I was trying to screw him out of his inheritance or something."

Priya's mouth fell open. "I will kill that man myself. What the hell is wrong with him?"

"I don't know. Maybe the same thing that was wrong with me, my mother, and my father. He was trying to be understood and going about it in all the wrong ways."

"There's nothing wrong with you."

"Are you sure about that? Because I feel like there is."

"There's not. I promise. You're just trying to find your way through. And I'm really sorry I haven't been around for it. But anytime you need me, you just get on a plane, okay?'

"You got it. Do you want me to drive you to the airport tomorrow morning?"

Priya glanced down quickly. "Hush now, you need to act all heartbroken and sad that I'm leaving. As a matter of fact, you are too sad to drive me. And that way Tyce will have to take me."

I laughed. "What's your big plan? To stalk him on the FDR and bang his brains out?"

She grinned. "God girl, I love how you think. That idea makes me happy, but why haven't I thought of that before? Oh my God, am I losing my edge?"

I snorted a laugh. "Oh my God, I really am going to miss you."

"And I'm going to miss you. But the real question is what are you going to do about Evan?"

"Well, I think Blake Security has pretty much cleared him. They still have some suspicions, but I think he's okay. They'll see. I don't believe Evan would ever hurt me. As for my Dad, I'm not really speaking to him at the moment, so I'm giving him lots of space."

"Yeah, okay, that's fair. But you know what? You're going to have to talk to him eventually."

"Why?"

"Because he's your father. Because you work with him. And also because your love of what you do came from him. So, no matter what he's done, he gave you some good things."

God, I hated it when she was right.

Oskar

I had taken over the kid's suite. And so far, I didn't think he minded too much. At that point, I was considering moving a cot in there. "How do you feel about a roommate?"

Matthias glared at me from around the monitor on the desk at the opposite side of the room. "Oi, mate, you have your own room, and your wife is in there waiting for you. Do you mind?"

"I'm not leaving until I know what the fuck is going on."

"Mate, we're all working on it, round the clock. You don't have to do this by yourself. As a matter of fact, let me take the burden."

I lifted a brow, ignored him, and went back to it. I was missing something, I could tell.

"You know, I'm looking forward to getting my rooms back."

I pretended not to hear him. "I have been over these numbers again and again. Livingston Perfumes' finances look good. The father's personal finances look good. The mother has been to rehab, all paid for by the family accounts which are more than healthy."

"Mate, I get it. Your in-laws have loot."

I frowned. In-laws. Why hadn't I really thought about that? Hailey was... Jesus Christ, some kind of an insane heiress.

The thing was I liked money. I loved money. I loved what money could buy, what it could give you access to. Most of the money I had accumulated before I turned twenty was... not always above board. And to be honest, when I'd come to work for Noah I'd kept it, and it had grown. I had a Midas touch when it came to money. But even the funds I'd accumulated didn't touch the kind of money Hailey's family had. "I don't care about their loot. She could walk away from all of it, and I'd be fine."

Matthias rolled his eyes. "That's because you know how to make that shit grow on trees."

"Yeah, I do." I grinned. "What I don't know how to grow on trees are fucking answers."

Matthias sighed and leaned back, rocking in his chair. "Look, I get it, what it's like going through hell, thinking you failed the woman you love. But shit, mate, if I can figure it out, you can figure it out."

"So you're saying you're the bigger disaster?"

Matthias just shrugged. "Remember that whole *I like to kill people* thing? And no, I didn't actually decide that, but someone put it in my head. And let's not forget that *my dad formed ORUS* thing either."

In terms of fucked-up scenarios, Matthias had the worst. His father had been one of the original founders of a shady government organization known as ORUS. Of course, he hadn't known that was his father until just recently. His own father had had him recruited from a really young age to be groomed and trained to kill people, and that wasn't some fucked-up shit. I'd thought my dad was bad, but at least the old man hadn't made me kill anyone.

What was worse was that while he was going to training, he had been subjected to some serious mind-control shit. It was a wonder the guy wasn't completely fucked in the head, but even he had managed to find someone to love him and to hold on to that person.

So maybe there is hope for you yet.

"How do you deal with it? Not knowing if she's safe?"

Matthias's eyes went somber as he leaned forward, dropping the front of his chair back to the ground. "I'm not going to lie, it's the worst. Knowing how often something could go wrong, I worry. Lots of worry. Sleepless nights. But then I remind myself that she's ORUS. She's just as well trained as I was. And considering she fought me hand to hand and lived to tell the tale, she's pretty bad ass. I just have faith she'll come back in one piece."

I shook my head. "Jesus Christ. I still can't believe your fiancé is ORUS. When is she going to leave the dark side?"

"She wants to fulfill her three-year contract. When she's done, she'll make her decisions. Noah, of course, already offered her a position here, but I don't want to push her. I want the choice to be hers. At the end of the day, it's her life. She's letting me share it with her. I don't get to dictate what she does."

I frowned. "Wouldn't it be easier if you just dictate it?"

Matthias laughed. "You've met Gemma, right? When was the last time anyone dictated anything to her?"

"Yeah, you have a point there, but I'm still not sure how you deal with knowing she puts herself in danger." Matthias's woman was next-level badass. All of the women in the house were, actually, but Gemma was the only one who had the full chops to back it up. Rafe's wife, Diana, was also a badass in her own right, but since getting pregnant, she'd had to slow down on her shenanigans. She'd hatched a whole revenge plot against Rafe only to discover that, well, like us, she'd been wrong about him. Then, of course, they had banged like rabbits. Much banging. Then they fell in love, he knocked her up, and now they were married. We were like some kind of insane, former-assassin dating agency.

"I find a way to deal with it, and then make that shit never about her. Because she's got a job to do, one she believes in, so I just have to deal."

The knot only tightened in my stomach. "It's so fucking hard."

"Yeah, mate. If it was easy, any big German idiot could do it." He winked at me.

I rolled my eyes and mumbled. "I think I liked it better when you never smiled."

Then his face broke into a broad, wide grin and I knew. "Your woman is standing right behind me, isn't she?"

The kid's eyes danced, and he clearly wasn't looking at me. I quickly saved my information and then stood, turning around. "Hey, Gemma. Welcome back, beautiful."

As always, Gemma had a smile for me. "Hello, you beautiful man." She gave me a big hug, and I wrapped my arms around her tight, holding on for just a second too long. Quick as a flash, that side of Matthias that he had a good firm handle on these days flashed in his eyes, and I knew it was time to let go. I stepped back. "Good to see you in one piece."

"Good to be back." Her gaze darted to Matthias. "Hey, baby."

His eyes said it all. *Come over here and fuck me senseless, and let's fill the whole house with your screams.*

That was my cue. "And I'll just leave you two crazy kids to it."

What the hell was I doing there anyway? Matthias was

right. I'd found the woman of my dreams. I couldn't let the fear of what might happen to her if I couldn't protect her lock me up. I couldn't let the fear of her waking up and realizing that I was the lucky one in our relationship stop me from being with her. I just prayed to God that I'd be able to hold on to her when this was all over.

CHAPTER SIX

———————

Oskar

"Hailey?" I called out for her when I opened the bedroom door.

"I'm in here," she called from the bathroom.

I don't know why, but I was so relieved to find her in here. It wasn't like she was going to run.

She smiled up at me in the mirror with a soft expression as she slathered lotion on her arms. "Hey, you. Where have you been?"

The hit of fear knotted my gut again. I loved her so

much. What if I couldn't keep her safe? What if I couldn't hold on to her?

You have her now. Hold her.

"Just working. Here, let me help you with that."

She giggled. "That look in your eyes tells me you have no intention on helping."

"I've always said you were intuitive, butterfly."

With a frustrated growl, I bent down to pick her up, placing her on the counter so that we were aligned. *Yes.* The way I lined up right against her sweet center made my eyes cross.

She rocked her hips into me, and I growled, giving her hair a little tug. Just the gentlest reminder that I wanted to control the pace. She made me feel like a damn caveman... or a Viking.

I pulled back and muttered, "Fuck." She had no idea what she was doing to me. Too fast and she wouldn't be ready, and I needed to make love to her. I needed this. I needed *her*. I didn't want to scare her off, and I didn't want to hurt her, but my control was thin at best. And fear was dissolving it quickly.

Hailey tugged up my T-shirt and slid her hands over my skin, tracing her fingertips over each abdominal muscle. I squeezed my eyes shut tight, trying to think of something, anything, to not lose control. I wanted to show her how much I loved her.

She dragged her hands up over my pecs and let them flutter down as she explored each ridge of muscle and bone. She placed her hand over my heart, and she sat there for a moment, letting our pulses synchronize.

Somehow that small act was the hottest thing she could have done in the moment, as if she sensed that I was terrified. My cock fought against my sweatpants, begging for release. It wanted to get out, to get closer to her. Inside her.

"Hailey, butterfly... need to slow down. If we don't—"

She sighed, and the sound went straight to my dick, doing nothing to cool the damn thing off. "I missed you tonight, that's all."

I wasn't sure if I should laugh or kiss her again. But as she took her time exploring my muscles, my skin vibrated with need. Electricity skipped over my arms, making the hairs stand up and my skin buzz. I tightened my jaw in a desperate attempt to regain control.

One of her fingers traced over the elastic of my waistband, and I held my breath. If she went down there, there was no telling what my dick would do. Instead, I quickly snapped my hand gently around both her wrists. "I'm warning you, Hailey. I'm too wound up. Too fast and you'll be walking funny for a week." I muttered, my voice all gravel and stone.

She met my gaze levelly, then her eyes traced over my chest again, down to my dick. She watched the action going on under my sweatpants for a long moment before tracing her gaze right back up again to meet my eyes. "Explain how that's a problem? I think I might like that."

What—? She wanted it fast? Raw? "Butterfly..."

"Well." She rocked her hips into me again and wrapped her arms around me. "Why don't you tell me what the problem is? You seem so tense. Maybe I could do something to take away that tension."

With every rock of her hips, my dick got a taste of the heat that was behind her yoga pants, and I wanted in.

I wanted her so bad I couldn't see straight. How the hell could I explain this? I could hardly say, 'You are being naughty.'

Oh yeah, she had my number. I slid my hands into her hair, angled her head, and kissed her. Gone were the tender kisses of earlier, the slow, leisurely licks. Instead, now I plundered, took full control, owning the moment. All with that one kiss.

She gasped. My thumb rested right at the juncture of her pulse, and I could feel her erratic heartbeat. Skipping ahead, running, running, running, racing. The problem was all my best intentions went to hell when she made that whimpering sound at the back of her throat. She wanted me as much as I wanted her.

Fuck it. I had to touch her. I lifted the hem of the T-shirt that she'd been wearing all day, and I splayed my hand around her tiny waist. God, she was so petite. *Be careful with her.*

She tore her lips away from mine and gasped on a breath. "Oskar."

I took the opportunity to kiss along the column of her throat to the delicate skin of her ear and laved it with my tongue. She tasted even better here. I wanted to reexamine exactly how she tasted all over. I wanted to rediscover exactly how she felt coming around my cock.

When I slid my hands up her torso, her breasts filled my

palms, and I groaned. Jesus. I rolled her nipples between my thumbs and forefingers, and Hailey threw her head back. "I— Oh God."

I growled and tugged her T-shirt up and over her head, tossing it to the floor. I had to see— Oh, shit. She was so fucking pretty. Full breasts that fit into my hand well. Pink, rosy nipples. All that smooth, tawny skin with the occasional freckle here or there. "You are so fucking perfect."

"I—please."

I leaned her back over the counter, shoving the products aside as I leaned over her, my mouth at the perfect height for her breasts. As I teased one nipple with my thumb and forefinger, gently rolling it back and forth, plucking the bud until it peaked, I wrapped my lips around the other one and sucked.

Hailey's back bowed, and she slid her hands into my hair and tugged. The motion made me want to bury myself deep inside her. Quick, swift, snug, and tight. Fuck. It hadn't been long enough. She couldn't possibly be ready. I'd made love to her that morning. I should have had better control.

More foreplay. More fucking foreplay. I switched to the

other breast. Teasing the one I just made wet with my mouth. Her hips continued to rotate into my cock, making it hard enough to cut diamonds.

She tried to tug my T-shirt over my head, and I paused my suckling only to give her what she wanted. She yanked the thing over my back, over my head, and then threw it to match the other T-shirt I'd tossed on the floor. Fuck.

God, I wanted to feel her breasts pressed into my chest as I lifted her slowly over my dick, over and over and over again. Yeah, that's what I wanted.

But first, I needed to taste her. Needed to see her melt apart on my tongue. I wanted her to see me now, not the man who left her all those years ago. Releasing her nipple with a loud popping sound, I kissed my way down her torso.

Her breath was short and panting, and she gasped my name over and over again, occasionally punctuated with *yes, more.*

When I reached her belly button, I dipped my tongue inside, teasing the sensitive spot until she giggled. Then I tugged down the elastic of her yoga pants, kissing the flesh that was exposed, inch by inch. When I yanked them off, I stared at the feast before me. Holy cow. She was so perfect. Sweet, wet, pink lips. And she was waxed. Not entirely, though, she'd left a thin strip like an arrow pointing the way. As if I could ever get lost. But God, I could already see her dewy wetness over her slick flesh.

"Widen your legs for me."

"What?" she whispered.

"You heard me. Legs wider. I want to see you."

She hesitated. "I, I don't—"

"I said, open your legs."

She gave me another shaky breath, but then she parted her thighs wider. I knelt in front of her and then pressed my lips on her skin, laving her slick flesh from clit to dewy center.

"Oh, shit." She flung an arm over her eyes as her other hand slid into my hair, helping guide me, showing me what she liked, when to stop, when to keep doing exactly what I was doing. Yeah, she liked that.

Against her flesh, I muttered, "You want to know how

you taste? Like the fucking sweetest silk I've ever tasted in my life. Buttery soft, and so good. So, so, good."

For several moments, all that could be heard was the whisper of my name on her tongue and her murmurs of appreciation as I continued to lick, taste, and tease. She melted on my tongue, melted just for me. And then her fingers clutched tight into my hair.

"Oh my God. I, I'm going to—"

I worked my tongue deep inside her, holding her hips steady as she rocked them on my tongue. Over and over and over again, as the waves overtook her. Yes. That's what I wanted. Her coming on my tongue, my fingers, my cock.

Another orgasm wracked her body, and this time, her hips lifted. And I held her tight to me as she melted. I continued to gently, slowly lick the sweet dew from her flesh. All the while, I took a thumb and teased that tight patch of skin just below her center. "Yeah, that's it. Open up for me."

One of her legs locked around my head for a third time, and her scream echoed through the bathroom. I smiled against her lips, and gave her one more long, leisurely lick, before brushing my lips along the inside of her thighs and kissing my way back up her body.

Her eyelids fluttered briefly, and the gaze she gave me was sleepy and half-lidded. "Oh my God."

"You okay?" I asked as I held back a chuckle. I loved that look on her face, though. It was perfect.

"Am I okay? I don't think I've ever, ever been more okay in my life."

I grinned. "In that case, let me help you feel even more okay." I picked her up and carried her into the bedroom. The whole time, she giggled and told me to put her down, that she could walk under her own steam.

"Not on your life."

When we reached the bed, I held her by the hips and deposited her gently in the center. Then I shucked my sweatpants, before reaching over to the bedside table for a condom. Hailey's eyes immediately went to my dick. Instead of that slightly panicked look, she licked her lips.

"Woman, keep looking at me like that and I'm going to show you what to do with that tongue."

"I'm pretty sure I know what to do." She reached out

tentatively, and gently ran her finger over the top of my dick, rubbing in the drop of moisture.

Fuck. I was going to come. Just like that. And all it took was one touch.

Shit. If she kept doing that, I was really going to. But I watched, fascinated as she licked her lips.

The look she gave me was shy, and even in the dim light of my room, I could see the slight flush on her cheeks. "Do you mind?" she asked softly.

Mind? Was she kidding? I shook my head. "No. I definitely do not mind."

We shifted positions, and I lay back against the pillows as she crawled over me. Teeth grazing her bottom lip, she watched me, assessed me. When she reached out a hand and wrapped it around the base of my dick, I couldn't hold back the string of curses. My accent was nearly American, but when she did this to me, all I could remember was German.

Jesus Christ, that felt incredible. Her delicate hands didn't even reach around me, but when she used both of them, it worked just fine. And then she leaned over and licked my head clean, and I knew I was lost.

Her lips wrapped around me, and I squeezed my eyes shut, trying desperately to hold on to the reins of control that were slipping freely out of my fingers. She bobbed her head down, taking me as far back as her throat would allow, and then she did the most incredible thing. She inhaled and relaxed her throat, taking me even farther.

Ah fuck, I was too close to coming. The tightening of my balls, the need for release building at the base of my spine. My muscles went taut, and I wanted to be inside her. I didn't want to come in her mouth.

Okay, who the fuck was I kidding? Yes, I did, but before that, I wanted to be inside her.

Taking a tight rein on my controls, I gently tugged her head back. "Baby, wait. Hailey, Jesus, you have to stop. I am going to come if you keep doing that."

She blinked at me, eased back off my cock, and said, "But I was busy."

Yes, yes she was. But I wanted to be inside her. Shit. Choices. But I stuck to my guns. Gently I rolled her onto her back. Then, I reached for the condom I'd dropped on the top of the nightstand. I tore the thing open with my teeth before rolling onto my side to glide it on. When I repositioned myself between her thighs, she gazed up at me and rubbed a thumb over my cheek.

"Oskar—"

With gritted teeth, I wrapped my hand around the base of my cock and gently guided it to her. With the tip, I teased over her slit again and again, making sure to tease her clit, making sure she was just as desperate I was. She was so wet.

With the tip of my cock nudging her tight entrance, I took a deep breath, met her gaze, and slid inside.

Her eyes went wide, and she held on to my shoulders, her nails biting into my skin.

"Fuck. Hailey."

She lifted her hips, taking me another inch deeper. For several minutes, I inched forward, and withdrew again, gritting my teeth. I teased her nipples and kissed her deep, making sure she still rode the waves of pleasure. When I slid back in, I knew I was hitting exactly the spot she needed, because her eyes rolled back, and her spine arched into every deep stroke.

"Hailey. So tight—so fucking—good." Her body snug around me, I let myself go. I let myself whisper all the things I dreamt about doing. How long I'd been dreaming of doing it, how bad I wanted her. How much I wanted to feel her come all over me.

"I, it feels so—oh, my God—" I couldn't form the words I wanted to say. Instead of 'I love you. I'm scared I can't protect you,' what I said was, "I need you so much."

I deliberately slowed my stroke on each retreat, where the head of my cock hit that little bundle of nerves deep inside. And then I would hitch forward just a tad, before fully retreating out again. Every time I did that, she gave me a low, primal moan.

"You like what I'm doing?" I punctuated the question with a kiss to her throat.

"I like it."

I reached underneath her, cupping her ass with one hand, and then flipping us over so she sat on top of me. "Show me how much you like it."

This way she could control the penetration. And bonus, I could watch her. I cupped her breast with one hand, taking one of her nipples between my fingers, as my other hand occupied itself with sliding over her clit. I knew what my job was. My job was to make her come as often as possible and make her come hard.

Hailey threw her head back. "Oh, my God, I, I'm going to—"

I gritted my teeth. Her inner muscles clamped tight around my cock, and I shuddered as her whole body shook over mine. Not yet. Not yet. Not. Fucking. Yet. She dropped her hands and propped herself up on my chest with them. I reached around her, cupping her ass, helping her move. With every uptick of my hips, her eyes rolled to the back of her head.

I could feel her, this was it. She was going to come again. With a curse, I gripped her hip with my free hand and held on for dear life as she exploded around me one last time. Her body went limp above me, but I didn't let her rest. Instead, I flipped us both back over so she lay on her back again, panting, every breath making her breasts bounce, drawing my attention.

I took both of her wrists in one hand, splayed her legs wide, and I drove deep. Deeper, and deeper, my thumb rubbing furiously on her clit, drawing out her orgasm, her body jerking beneath mine. And then it hit me with the force of a tidal wave. The orgasm wound around my spine, ricocheting through my body, making me explode into a thousand tiny shards.

Holy shit. My wife was going to kill me.

***

Oskar

I was in the gym when I heard the commotion. The cussing, screaming, and then the scuffling. I could hear Noah's voice calling for Jonas. Then I heard Rafe's voice. "Fuck. Someone get Oskar down here."

I grabbed a towel and wiped it down my face as I tugged open the door to the gym. "What the fuck is going on?"

It only took me three steps to see. Elijah was back, and he was scuffling with Noah and Rafe, determined to get past them. Either one of them could have put him down on his back in zero time flat, but they were very deliberately trying not to hurt him.

"What the fuck? What is happening here?"

Elijah jammed a finger toward me. "You, you thieving asshole."

"Excuse me?"

"You've stolen everything I have worked for."

I put my hands up. He may had been Hailey's father, but the guy was an off his rocker. "I promise you, when I steal from you, you will know it. You will feel it to the core of your center. I haven't taken a dime from you."

"You stole my baby."

A chill washed over me. I could feel hooks grabbing onto my spine, refusing to let go. Fuck, he knew. "Wait just a minute there."

And then I saw it, the slight smirk on Rafe's face. He could have held on to the guy. Noah was still in don't-hurt-the-client mode, but Rafe just let his hands slip, and Elijah rushed forward. I still had my hands up. I could deck him, but he was an old man, and also, Hailey's father. So when I saw the punch coming, there wasn't much I could do. I wasn't going to duck and run, not from him. Not from anybody. But I couldn't hit him back. So, I let it come, right in the fucking kisser.

Son of a bitch, that hurt.

When was the last time I'd taken a pop to the face? *The last time one of your partners tried to kill you.* Right. That shit needed to stop happening. My pretty mug couldn't take it.

"Are you happy now?"

"No." He wound up another fist, but this one I caught and gently deflected. But even as gently as I could, it was with enough force that he stumbled, so then I had to catch him. That's when Hailey came out, robe wrapped around her, silk head scarf still on.

"Dad? What is going on here? It's barely six in the morning."

"Hailey, get your things young lady. We are leaving."

She raised her brow. "What?"

"You heard me. I said get your things. We are leaving."

Hailey crossed her arms. "I think you have forgotten that, A, I am not a child, B, you are not in charge of me, and C, you have no right to tell me what to do with my life."

Her father sputtered and then turned his attention on me. "You were supposed to keep her safe. But no, you were just trying to get your hands on my money." He turned his eye on Noah then. "You say you help people. Don't think I haven't heard the whispers that you do other things. How the hell does a security agency manage the most expensive real estate in Manhattan?"

I plunged in then. I knew I should keep my mouth shut, but my lips were still throbbing from that cheap shot. "I happen to be very good with money."

He aimed again, and again I deflected and then caught him before he fell and hurt himself.

I didn't dare look at Hailey. I was too afraid of what she'd say.

But she jumped in the fray. "You will stop this nonsense right now. I am a guest here. I will not outstay my welcome."

"Baby, you're always welcome here."

"You married him." Her father spat.

Hailey inhaled a deep breath. "Yes, in Vegas. Years ago, I didn't even remember, I guess, but that's not the point. The point is, Oskar and I," she slid her gaze to me and a small smile played on her lips, "are happy. And even if this all happened by accident, it is a good thing. It doesn't matter if we're married or not. He has money of his own. He doesn't need any of mine."

"You mean, any of mine. You don't have your inheritance yet."

Hailey held herself still. I could see the ice that was growing in her, building, snapping, re-growing thicker and stronger, refortifying. She tipped her chin up. "You can keep every dime. I'm smart. You need me more than I need you. I receive offers to work for competing companies every day, but I am a Livingston. The company is my home. You can choose to fire me. You can choose to withhold my inheritance. But you will not take my name. You will not take who I am. Even after everything you have lied to me about, this is your choice. I made my choices, and I'm sticking with them."

Elijah was having none of it, and he stepped into her space.

I immediately stepped between them. "Elijah, enough."

He glared up at me. "You will step aside."

When I didn't budge, he leaned around me. "You are just like your mother. Flighty. You have no idea what the real world is about."

Hailey said something I didn't think she had in her.

"Which mother? The one who raised me, or the one you paid off after your adulterous affair?"

Rafe hissed. Noah ducked his head and shook it. I wanted to grin but held it together for the most part.

Elijah staggered back. "I do not expect to see you in the office today."

"In order for that to happen, you'll have to actually fire me. And if you're not prepared to do that right now, I'll see you when I see you."

Her father sputtered and blustered before marching out.

I turned to face her slowly. "Jesus Christ, I am married to a badass."

Her face fell as she took in my appearance. "Oh my God, did he hit you?"

I shrugged. "Yeah, it hurts a lot. I think you need to kiss it better."

Her brow rose suspiciously, so I tried to wipe the leer off my face and look sad and pathetic.

She shook her head. "Rafe, Noah, did my father actually hit him?"

Rafe, the idiot, laughed. "Yeah, it was awesome. I'm pretty sure Matthias caught that on camera somewhere here. We can replay it for movie night."

Noah chuckled. "It was a cheap shot, and Oskar let him do it."

She slid her glance back to me. "Why would you let him hit you?"

"Because he's your father, and I have been defiling his daughter. Repeatedly."

Rafe made gagging noises from the foyer. "Eww. It's bad enough to hear you two at night, but to hear you actually say it, that's just gross."

Noah chuckled and dragged Rafe back into the conference room. "Will you two get a room?"

I laughed. "This, coming from you? I have seen your wife's bare ass more than I've seen my own in the last month."

I heard the growl first, and then Rafe was holding Noah back. I took Hailey's hand and pulled her with me. "Look, you need to work things out with your dad."

"No, he needs to apologize, and until then, I will work as

normal. But I'm not working anything out with him."

I knew that this situation was going to take some time, so I shifted gears. "I mean, he did hit me in the face, so I feel like I deserve some compensation by a member of the Livingston family."

She laughed. "Oh yeah?"

"Yeah. And the thing is, the pain... it migrates."

Hailey snorted and then giggled loud enough that it ricocheted off the walls of the penthouse. "Oh really? Just where did it migrate to?"

With her hand in mine, I slid it over my chest to my heart. "Right here."

She stopped and gave me a soft, sweet smile, before leaning forward and pressing a kiss to my pec. "There, all better?"

I gave her another leer. "Yeah, but now it's moved again."

And this time, when I moved her hand, her pupils dilated and she shook her head. "Do you realize, we're going to have to work out some kind of arrangement so I'm not late to work every day of my life?"

"I think we can work something out."

CHAPTER SEVEN

Hailey

Despite Oskar's attempts to distract me, I was still fuming over what my father said. Flighty? No one ever accused me of being flighty in my life. I was the serious one who always focused on work. How could he call me flighty?

Oskar kissed my neck, his hands sliding up my belly to cup my breasts. "Sweetheart, I'm going to need you to focus now, okay?"

"Yeah, okay, I'm focused."

He chuckled low as he nipped my ear. "No, you're not.

You have a hand on my dick and you're not squeezing it, or moving it, or anything. That's just teasing it."

"Sorry, yes, of course. Let's have sex."

He laughed and then nipped my ear. "As much as that sounds like fun, you're clearly upset. Now, my preferred method of distraction is sex, but maybe we should just talk about what just happened?"

I turned around in his arms. "He called me flighty."

"Butterfly, anyone who knows you knows you're not flighty, okay?"

"No, not okay, because how could he say that to my face? I'm the one who's been running the company. He's given me more and more responsibility, and I've taken it on without complaint. The shareholder meetings, the marketing strategies, I'm doing the work. I'm running the company, and he has the nerve to call me flighty? He's the one who had an affair and then tried to pass off his love child. Who does that?"

Oskar shrugged. "My guess is a surprising number of people."

"Are you serious right now?"

He held me tight, sliding his hands down over my ass and bringing me up against him. "Yes, this is my serious face." His expression evened out. And there was not a single hint of a smile anywhere. For once, he actually did look serious. What was always so fascinating was that while everyone said he scowled a lot, I was used to him teasing and smiling. But yeah, this face was foreboding.

"That's a good serious face."

He nodded solemnly. "Now, can you please put your focus where it matters? On my dick?" And then he flashed a grin.

I slapped his shoulder. "Don't be a jackass."

The laugh tumbled from his lips easily. "Come on, I'm only teasing. My dick can wait. Unless of course you *want* to touch it right now, in which case, he is always ready."

Then to punctuate that point, the hard length of him twitched against my thigh. Dear God, the man was always ready.

"No, I don't feel like touching your dick right now. Okay, I might feel like touching it, but I'm mad right now. I don't think you want me to."

He nuzzled my nose with his. "Newsflash, Butterfly. I don't care how mad you are. I always want you to touch my dick. You can touch it in anger. You can touch it in sadness. You can touch it when you're happy. Touch it all the time. As a matter of fact, never stop touching it."

"Yeah, that would make it difficult to get anything done around here."

"Hey, it happens. It wouldn't be the first time any one of us has seen dick touching before. I promise."

"Can you be serious?"

"Okay, I'm sorry." He rubbed my back gently. "Your father is upset. He knows that he owes you an apology, but he doesn't know how. He knows he lied. He knows he's wrong. And he's angry with himself. Either he doesn't recognize it yet or doesn't know how to deal with it and make amends, so he's lashing out. Right now, that's you. You and I both know you haven't done anything wrong. You're the least flighty person I know. You're confident and smart, and you have this insanely adorable nose, which is actually very useful." He kissed the tip of my nose and I wiggled it. "And you also have a big heart. You encased it in ice because your whole life, people didn't always show you the love that you deserved. But your father wasn't one of those. He's always loved you. And you knows he loves you now. He just doesn't know how to come out and say he's sorry."

"When did you get so sensitive?"

"Hey, don't tell the guys, okay? You're going to ruin my rep."

I laughed. "You know what, I think I'm going to take the day off."

He grinned. "That's the spirit. We could spend the day in bed, me inside you, Netflix and chilling."

I laughed. "Um, if you're inside me, we're definitely not chilling."

"Sure, we could be. Like a comfort thing. You know, I'll just brush your nipples, screw you nice and slow. We'll have Netflix on the background. That's enough for some chilling, right?"

I shook my head. "Oh my God, I can't with you right now. Don't you have a job to go do?"

"Well, sorry sweetheart, but if you're here I'm here, seeing as I'm on guard duty today. So take off all your clothes."

"Oh my God. I think I'm just going to get some rest, catch up on some meetings, relax. You, go. Didn't I hear something about Rafe having a job?"

He scowled then. "Yeah, I owe that motherfucker one."

"Play nice."

"What do you mean play nice? He let your father go so he could hit me."

I chuckled. "Are you sure he let him go? My father can be very wily."

"Rafe was a goddamn assa—" He cut himself off.

"Rafe was a what?"

He sighed. "An FBI agent. There's no way he let him go by accident."

"Okay, but why don't you still go do the job. I'm taking up enough of your time. Besides, this place is a fortress, and nothing bad can happen to me here."

"So now is not the time to tell you that we've had a couple of break-ins here?"

My mouth fell open. "What?"

He shook his head. "Never mind. We have adjusted the security parameters since then. It's fine. Totally fine."

"No, who the hell broke in here?"

He sighed. "One time, Rafe broke in here. But that was when he was convinced that Noah was a bad guy, and he was trying to save Lucia from Noah."

I frowned as I tried to piece those things together. "So, he broke in here?"

Oskar nodded. "Yeah, long story. But we're all good now. Well, obviously, Noah and Lucia are married and they have Izzy, so yeah. Oh, and I guess Gemma broke in here once before too."

I stared at him. "The gorgeous redhead? How did she break in here?"

"Another long story. But we're all brothers now."

"Why don't you head out and go to work? I'm going to get some rest, okay? I want to try and forget everything that has happened and figure it out from here, okay?"

"Are you sure?"

"Yeah, I'm sure."

"Okay, if you need anything, just text me. I'll come right back."

I watched as he left. *How is it that I've fallen in love with him in such a short span of time?*

Oskar

"That our guy?"

Rafe pulled off the binoculars. "No, our guy has got a tattoo right there on his neck."

I rolled my eyes and tried to adjust the seat further back. "Because nothing says classy like neck tattoo."

Rafe chuckled. "Hey, don't yuck somebody else's yum. Some women think neck tattoos are hot."

"Lots of guys in prison think neck tattoos are hot too."

Rafe snorted at that. "How's your lip pretty boy?"

I scowled at him. He honestly shouldn't poke me, considering he was the reason I had a split lip in the first place.

"You're an ass."

"What? He got around me." He shrugged. "Also, you are married to his daughter and didn't think to mention it to him, so, there's that."

"I didn't know until we took the job, dumbass."

"Yeah, but he didn't know that. And, let's face it, after all the shit you've given me over the years, you had it coming."

"If you want to tussle with me, we can tussle anytime."

Rafe grinned. "Oh, you mean like the last time?"

"You ambushed us! You want a fair fight?"

I knew I was asking for it. I was good in a fight. I was. It was a by-product of being around unsavory people all my life. But Rafe was better. He had full-on killer instinct. As in, the motherfucker could kill easily kill you just as soon as you got near him.

"All right. I'm sorry. The big bad German got his lip cut. Do you need a cuddle?"

I grinned at him. "Oh, I already got one."

Rafe shuddered. "Gross."

I shifted my gaze through the windshield again. "I think that's him."

Rafe peered through the binoculars. "Yeah, that's him."

Rafe and I were out of the car in seconds. Elis Ramson, drug dealer and all-around douche, knocked his girlfriend around so bad that he put her in the hospital. She was too scared of him to report him to the police. But her mother wasn't scared of him, and she'd called us. It was our job to scare some Jesus into him.

And if we were lucky, he'd fight back so we could beat him so bad he'd learn that lesson hard and never be tempted to repeat it, ever again. Maybe we'd call cops. Not likely, but, maybe. It was weird. I was kind of looking forward to it. After all, I'd been tense for a while. The whole thing with Hailey, not being able to catch who was going after her... I needed to work some of that tension out, and this asshole was as good a way as any.

Rafe headed toward the alley in the back. I went to the front. I nodded my head at the bouncer, and he waived me through ahead of the line, much like he'd done for poor Elis. When we'd first arrived, we'd given him a C-note to not give us any bullshit at the door. Thanks to his girlfriend's mother, we knew that this was Elis's favorite watering hole and that he'd show up eventually. But given that he had a habit of hanging out with unsavory characters, there was a chance he'd cut and run. Hence, Rafe posted up at the back door in the alley.

When I rolled up to the bar, I saw he'd gotten himself a beer and a shot, and he slid me a glance. "I know you?"

I shook my head. "Nope." I signaled the bartender for a beer, although, chances were Elis would bolt before I'd even get a chance to drink it. I paid and then leaned against the bar, glaring at him. I'd perfected my glare. It usually scared assholes, but this guy stared me down. "I don't know you, but I know your girlfriend Maria. Got to tell you, she's real upset with your tendancy to go all Rocky Balboa on her."

What he should have done was shit himself. Instead, what he did was chuckle. "I didn't do anything to her that she didn't deserve."

The searing heat of anger flashed through me, white and hot and completely unrelenting. I hated assholes. I really did. Bullying assholes were the worst. I pushed to my full height and got real close. "You know what? I don't even get it. You're as ugly as fuck, motherfucker. It must have been a pity fuck."

Oh yeah, that did it. He slammed his bottle down. "Motherfucker, I will fuck you up—"

He didn't get to finish his line. Yeah, I popped him in the face. "Yeah, all that talking coming out of your ugly pie hole is annoying, so there's that."

He staggered back and pulled himself to standing. "I will fucking kill you." He tried with a wild swing, which I deflected, and then I popped him in the face again.

This time he came roaring at me, and I let him get just close enough. "Go on, I dare you. I can't wait for this to get really ugly, for the cops to come and then put you in lock up. Word is Luis Montoya has been dying to talk to you." That got him.

Thanks to Maria, we learned that Elis was also a thief. He had stolen from a jailer six months ago and done Montoya a nice frame up. He'd gotten him popped and locked up for four years. Montoya, obviously, had a grudge to repay. So if we weren't able to teach Elis a lesson, we'd let Montoya do it for us.

Apparently that terrified him, because instead of coming back at me, he bolted for the back door. I touched my com. "Coming your way, dick-head."

Rafe just chuckled. "Oh, I'm ready. I'm just waiting on you. Are you going to finish your drink first? What did you get, an appletini?"

"That shows what you know. I got a Bellini. I happen to like them. Peach is yummy."

I could hear Rafe chuckle and then the sound of the back door slamming open. I took my time. I had to let Rafe have his fun. I trusted that he knew not to kill the asshole. Although, sometimes those ORUS instincts kick in at the worst times.

I shoved open the back door, and Rafe had the poor kid on his face, a knee in his back, and Elis was begging for his life, begging not to be sent to lock-up. Rafe leaned forward. Gone was his former cover, the FBI agent. This guy was a lot worse. He looked like he was enjoying himself.

Rafe just grabbed his hair then slammed his face into the concrete.

"All right, all right. You got to keep him pretty. I feel like Montoya is going to want him pretty for what he has planned for him."

Rafe laughed. "You know what? That's a good point. We won't call the cops for—"

The hairs on my neck stood at attention right before I heard the crack of a gunshot, and then there was fire. Fire racing up my arm, bursting through my chest. I could feel it. Fuck, that burned. Why was I on fire?

Suddenly, everything felt heavy, so goddamn heavy.

I could hear Rafe shouting at me. "Fuck. Motherfucker, wake up."

But the more he shouted, the more distant his voice was. Holy shit. I'd been shot.

I didn't know how much longer it was after that, but I was being lifted. God, I was really fucking on fire. Why did it burn so much? Rafe, the asshole, wouldn't leave my side. He applied pressure like a goddamn tourniquet. He took off his own belt. How bad was it? Shit, maybe I didn't want to know. I lifted my head. "If you're going to get naked, no thanks. I'd rather die."

"Shut up. I'm not letting you bleed out. I mean, you're annoying as fuck, but you're still my brother."

"Aww! I didn't know you loved me." I could have sworn I heard him mutter asshole, but that's all I remembered until we were back at the penthouse. I didn't remember much of the drive. I remembered nothing of what was said, and I had zero idea how the hell I got shot. But that was another problem for another day, I thought. The last thing I remembered before blacking the hell out, was Doc Breckner asking if there was anyone they should call for me. Rafe said something about someone getting Hailey the hell in there, but I grabbed his hand with my good arm. "No, not letting her... not... seeing... like this."

"You're an idiot, you know that?"

Yeah, I did know that. Everything went black.

CHAPTER EIGHT

Hailey

Work had always been my escape. From a young age, my parents knew that I had an unusually sensitive nose, but that wasn't the only part of the business that I loved.

Losing myself in scents, testing them, trying new combinations and then deciding how to market them was really fun, that's true. But the marketing was almost as much fun. Taking an idea from the beginning stages all the way to launch filled me with pride every time. I think for years my father thought I was just humoring him when he taught me about the business side of the company, but I was always paying attention.

Every new product was like a child that had to be nurtured and encouraged. After the gala for the launch of Miriam, it was time for me to see my child's report card.

Hours went by as I reviewed the feedback our contacts submitted about the new perfume. Miriam was created with my mother's particular tastes in mind, but that didn't mean I didn't want it to be a commercial success also. Nothing would make me happier than my mom's namesake perfume becoming as iconic as Chanel No. 5.

I was so engrossed in the reports that hours went by before I looked up again. When I did, my neck creaked in protest. I rolled my shoulders, trying to get the kinks out after being propped in bed so long. How long had I been working? I glanced at my watch and then blinked, shocked at how much time had flown by. Oskar should have been back already. It was almost the end of the day.

I leaned over to get my phone out of my handbag. Nothing. No calls or messages. A sudden sense of unease tightened like a knot in my stomach. Then I laughed. How spoiled I'd become by Oskar's attention if one afternoon without him made me feel like this. He'd probably just gotten caught up working with Rafe. He hadn't mentioned what type of job it was, but it was highly likely they had run into some sort of complication and he just hadn't been able to call.

Just then there was a quick knock at the door. Startled, I sat up pulling the covers over me protectively. "Yes?"

The door opened. As soon as I saw Rafe standing there, I knew.

"Tell me he's okay."

Rafe sighed. "He's okay. But I need you to come with me."

Despite his words, the knot in my throat didn't subside. Rafe's presence meant that Oskar wasn't well enough to come fetch me himself, which was saying something right there. I stuck my feet into the slippers next to the bed, my mind racing the whole time. Was Oskar really okay, or was that just Rafe's way of keeping me calm for now? I followed Rafe quietly down the hallway and into a back section of the penthouse I'd never seen before. We turned into a room that was set up like a hospital with several beds and fluorescent lighting. Oskar was on one of the beds, his eyes closed and his face pale.

"Oh no! Oskar!" I rushed to his side, hesitating before

putting my hand gently on his arm. At my touch, his eyes fluttered and then opened.

"Hey, butterfly."

A million emotions crashed over me at the same time. Relief, joy, then confusion and anger. I wanted to hug him and also rail at him for having the nerve to get hurt. But instead, I leaned down and kissed his forehead.

"You scared me."

He chuckled, pausing to cough so violently that it hurt me to hear it. I looked behind me frantically. There was a small cup of water with a straw on the table next to him, so I picked it up and brought it carefully to his lips. He took a few sips before collapsing back against the pillows. I could see how much that small effort had taken out of him.

"What happened?"

He shrugged. "I got the bad guy. Just happened to get in the way of a bullet while doing it."

I swayed slightly. "You got shot?"

His trademark smirk appeared. "It's just a scratch."

It should have been out of place on his face while he was

so pale and tired, but ironically it calmed me down. This was the Oskar I knew, always a smartass.

"I think you and I have different ideas about what a scratch is, but that's another story."

"It's not so bad if it's got you by my side smiling at me. My butterfly."

That was when I noticed the slight slur to his words and the loopy way he was smiling. I laughed and brushed his hair back from his face.

"Oh, they've got you on the good stuff, huh? I bet I could ask you anything right about now and you'd tell me."

He let out a long sigh. "Don't be mad at me. I never want you to be mad at me."

I squeezed his hand and withdrew, thinking that it was time to track down Rafe or someone who knew what to do with all this medical stuff. If Oskar was high as a kite right now, he certainly couldn't tell me what had happened to him or what should be done for his care. But before I could move away, Oskar grabbed my hand again.

"Don't go. I don't want you to go."

Alarmed at the desperation in his voice, I moved back to

his side, as close as I could get with the handles up on the medical bed.

"I'm not going anywhere. Sshh."

But nothing I said seemed to penetrate. Oskar brought my hand to his mouth and then pressed it to his cheek.

"I didn't want to leave you the first time. It was the hardest thing I've ever had to do."

I considered myself an ethical person. The man was drugged up and vulnerable, so it was completely wrong to let him spill his guts in this state. And under any other circumstances, I would never have allowed it. But then he said something that made it impossible for me to ignore.

"It was for your own good, you know. I had to leave for your safety."

When he looked up at me blearily, I decided that I wasn't as good of a person as I'd always hoped.

Oskar

She was so beautiful. Hailey had come into the room with a contrite Rafe right behind her, and I immediately had forgotten about the pain in my arm and my annoyance at being laid up.

Then I shifted on the uncomfortable hospital bed and lightning lanced through my arm.

"Fuck, this hurts."

Hailey made a little cooing sound and stroked my hair gently. It probably wasn't my manliest moment, but I'm pretty sure I whimpered. If I could have, I would have dragged her over the edge of the bed right then and put her right on top of me. But I couldn't.

Sine my arm was throbbing like a rotten tooth.

"I'm so glad you're here." I closed my eyes and had the uncomfortable sensation of floating away. Whatever Dr. Breckner had injected into my IV was fucking with my mind for sure, but I didn't even care. Hailey was here, which meant that all was finally right with the world.

"I never wanted to leave you."

"Then why did you?"

Her soft voice seemed to come from far away and I started to panic. Was she leaving me? Where was she going? I needed to keep her close. Keep her safe. I think I told her that but wasn't sure because the next thing I knew it was darker in the room and I was waking up.

"Hailey!"

She appeared at my side immediately. Her hair was standing up wildly on one side, and she blinked several times like she was just waking up.

"I'm here. Hey, I'm right here."

When her hand landed on my arm, I suddenly needed her to know. To understand.

"I had to keep you safe. I'm not a good man. Neither is my father. I would never want the sins of my past to touch you. You're so much better than that. So much better than me."

Hailey sniffled softly. "I wish you would have told me. Waking up alone hurt so much."

"Hurt is better than dead," I mumbled. Something in the back of my mind was shouting at me to shut the hell up, but I was in too much pain to listen. What had that voice ever done for me? Other than make me leave my butterfly behind and make us both unhappy.

"You should be free. I don't want to be the one to clip your wings."

Soft lips brushed against my cheek. "Your kind of sweet when you're drugged up, you know that?"

I tried to fight the current and open my eyes. If I could see her, then I could tell her to stop hitting my arm. But I couldn't.

The next thing I knew, bright light was in my face. I grunted at the piercing pain going through my skull.

"What the hell?"

There was a scuffle. Then I heard JJ's voice. "Jesus, don't just turn the lights on like that. The man is in a hospital bed. Even I'm not that cruel."

And just like that I was instantly awake. God knows I didn't want my health and well-being in the hands of nurse JJ. Just the thought was terrifying.

"What's going on?"

Rafe stood next to my bed scowling at me. "Finally. I thought you were going to sleep all day."

"Well, sorry to inconvenience you. Getting shot is no excuse for a sick day, huh?"

He grinned. "Glad you didn't die. Now can we move on?"

JJ laughed. "And you guys act like I'm the crazy one. Whatever. I'll go get Hailey. It took a lot of convincing to get her to leave to shower and get something to eat, but she'll kick my ass if I don't tell her you're awake."

Hearing Hailey's name brought a smile to my face. Then it dimmed. I remembered Hailey being here before. Wasn't I talking to her?

"What's that face for?" Rafe asked.

I glanced over at him in alarm. Just that quickly, I'd forgotten he was even here.

"Nothing. I just can't remember what happened. How long was I out?"

He shrugged. "Not that long. I was just giving you a hard time. It's been less than twenty-four hours. Hailey was right here with you the whole time, though. I really like her. She's the only one who can deal with your bullshit."

I flipped him off with my good hand. "Just wait until this arm heals."

He returned the middle finger salute as he walked out. Just after he cleared the doorframe, Hailey rushed in.

"You're awake." Her soft smile made me feel brand new. Had anyone ever been that happy to see me before?

She'd changed clothes and the hair around her temples looked damp. I couldn't stop staring at her.

"What? Do I have something on my face?" She swept a hand across her cheek self-consciously.

"You're perfect."

Hailey blushed, the very tops of her cheekbones turning pink. But I could tell that the compliment pleased her. I made a mental note to tell her every day.

"I never would have guessed you were so talkative while on pain meds, but I think I've learned more about you in one night than in the past few weeks."

"Why do you say that? What did I say?" The unease I'd felt earlier came back. This was why I'd never even wanted to do drugs. It wasn't a good idea to be that out of control. Not when you had the kind of secrets I did. In my world, loose lips got you killed.

"Just a bunch of stuff about how you left me for my own good. That you didn't want to, but it was the only way to keep me safe. Stuff like that."

I relaxed slightly. "Sounds like I was pretty high."

She shrugged. "Maybe, but you seemed very sure about what you were saying."

The blanket around my waist was suddenly very interesting. After I picked off a few loose threads, I looked up to see Hailey watching me closely.

Finally, she sighed. "So, are you finally going to tell me the truth or not?"

Apparently. my poker face wasn't as good as it once was. But hey, I wasn't exactly at my best after being shot and then dosed with narcotics to relieve the pain. But now my mind was clear, and I could probably come up with some kind of bullshit story that would throw her off the scent.

That's what the old me would have done. The Oskar that was used to hiding, twisting the truth, and staying one step ahead of danger. For the first time in my life, I didn't want to stay one step ahead. Being ahead kept you alive, but it also kept you alone. After working with the other guys at Blake Security, I'd gotten used to having a family of sorts to watch my back. I'd seen that it was possible to change your life completely and have the sorts of things I'd always assumed weren't meant for men like me. Family. Love. Hope. Stability.

All it would take was one leap of faith. But I still wasn't sure I was ready to let Hailey all the way in. Not just because of the danger but because I didn't want to see the moment she realized what kind of man she'd married.

Falling off the pedestal she'd put me on was going to hurt like a bitch.

"The truth doesn't always have a happy ending, baby."

She crossed her arms, hugging herself like she was trying to keep warm. "I know that. But there's no happy ending even possible when you're living a lie. At least give us a chance."

I sighed. "Come here. You might as well get comfortable. This is going to take a little while."

She climbed up on the hospital bed next to me and snuggled close. Once her head was nestled on my shoulder, her hand floated down to rest on top of my chest. I took a moment to just enjoy having her this close.

A few seconds later Hailey whispered, "This had better not be a ploy just to feel me up."

It felt good to laugh. Then I started talking.

CHAPTER NINE

Hailey

For a minute, Oskar was quiet. I thought he'd changed his mind when he took a deep breath.

"I came from a family of crooks. In fact, crook is probably a nice word for my father. He was more like a financial terrorist, but he cleaned up well and was clever enough to get away before any of his schemes blew up in his face. At least for a while. That's something we were both good at. Like father like son, I guess."

Listening is a skill. One that seems so simple. But it was taking all the willpower I had to remain still and let Oskar tell his story without interrupting. It was hard because I could hear the shame in his voice as he was talking. Almost as if he was expecting me to judge him.

"There is always a demand for people who have a talent with money. Numbers always came easily to me. Making money was like a game, one that I always won. And in the world I grew up in, it was natural that I'd work at my father's side. It wasn't long before I had a reputation for being just as thorough, just as aggressive. I had a client once that said watching us make money was like watching Jesus feed the masses with five loaves and two fish. We were like gods."

I tightened my arm around his middle. The world he described was nothing like anything I could understand. And despite the things he was saying, the idea of Oskar being in that world was just as strange. My Oskar? The wisecracking jerk who could drive me up the wall but was also willing take a bullet to protect someone else? The man I knew bore no resemblance to the one he was describing.

"The truth isn't what you expected, is it?" he asked quietly.

I had to be honest. "No. But that doesn't mean I don't want to hear it."

"Well, I guess I don't need to say too much more about my upbringing. I was raised by a bad man who taught me to be just like him."

"What about your mom? Did she know what was going on?" I was trying to be as matter of fact as he was, but my heart was breaking. He was calmly telling me that he'd been raised to be a moneymaker for criminals as if it was no big deal that his childhood had been stolen.

"My mother was a good woman. I think she tried to teach me as best she could, but she was as afraid of him as any of us were. She died when I was in college. Heart attack. I'm sure the stress of living with my father all those years was the real cause."

"I'm so sorry, Oskar."

"Me too. I wish I could have shown her that I wasn't like him before she died. She left this earth thinking that she'd failed me."

I sat up slightly, just so I could see his face. "I think she knew. I bet she could see the same things in you that I do. Underneath that tough guy act, there's a big, warm heart. I bet you got that from her."

He leaned forward, and I met him halfway, kissing

him sweetly, wishing that I could inject all my love for him into the embrace. I knew what he was doing with that story. He probably thought he was going to scare me off, and that just like everyone else in his life, I would abandon him once things got a little hard.

But Oskar had never experienced how stubborn a Livingston could be when we wanted something. He was my husband, and I wasn't going anywhere.

"What happened the weekend we met?"

He rested his forehead against mine. "I saw you and knew I had to have you. It was like getting punched in the gut. God, you were so beautiful even sitting at the bar wearing a fucking business suit."

His laugh made me chuckle too. I remembered being so annoyed that the assistant I'd brought with me to Vegas for a business conference had quickly ditched me to go drink with some random people she'd met.

"That wasn't exactly my scene for sure."

"I could tell. But you still outshone everyone else in the place. I'd just finished a job for one of my most influential clients. One so big that no one even says his name aloud. We just called him Mr. X. I was done and celebrating, and then I saw this angel. How could I resist?"

"And then you asked me why I was so pissed off?" I'd been so shocked that he was even talking to me. Oskar was gorgeous, and there had been plenty of women there that night watching him put away drinks.

"You looked so adorable drinking your one glass of wine with that haughty expression."

"It wasn't haughty. It was disappointed. I'd always heard so much about Vegas, and the reality was... underwhelming."

Oskar's gaze grew heated. "But I showed you a little excitement, didn't I?"

His hand, which had been resting at the small of my back, starting inching down until he had a good grip on my ass. I wiggled a finger at him.

"Uh-uh. Aren't you supposed to be recuperating?"

"I heal fast."

"Then tell me the rest of the story. After we boinked each other's brains out and got married, what happened before I woke up alone that Sunday?"

He sighed. "I went downstairs to get us some breakfast, and I saw Mr. X. He was there in Vegas."

"Oh, no. No wonder you didn't come back."

"There was no way I was going to lead him straight to you, Hailey. Men like that have no boundaries and no ethics. He would have used you as a pawn to get me to do what he wanted, which was to come work for him full-time."

"So you just disappeared."

"I disappeared. Noah had gotten me out of a few scrapes before. He was aware of my reputation and offered me a chance to use my skills legally. To help people. Plus, I knew that he had the skills to watch my back and keep certain people off my scent. With Noah and Matthias helping me, I could hide in plain sight. I just had to sacrifice the one thing I'd ever wanted to keep."

I shook my head. "You will never know how long I thought about you. How many nights I cried myself to sleep wondering what I'd done wrong. I felt so stupid. So naïve."

He kissed me again. "You were perfect. I was the problem."

"Believe it or not, it actually helps to know the whole story."

Oskar repositioned himself slightly but couldn't hide his wince. I sat up immediately. "Oh my god, you're hurt and here I am laying all over you!"

He smirked. "I kinda like you all over me."

"Only you can be a perv even when you're injured."

He glanced down at the huge tent in his blanket. "Not all of me is injured. Clearly."

Laughing, I climbed off the hospital bed and straightened the covers over him. Nothing could hide the huge lump, so I finally gave up. "Let me go ask if we can relocate you to your own room."

It took a little while, but finally I was able to locate Matthias. He followed me back to the medical bay and I waited outside while he talked to Oskar.

"You can go in now. I changed the dressing on the wound. As long as it's kept clean and dry, he'll be fine. He declined any more pain medication, but call me if he changes his mind."

He was gone before I could remind him that I didn't have

his number. Oh well, I would hunt him down physically if I thought Oskar needed the pills. He wouldn't ask for them, so I would have to watch him closely. If I thought he needed them, I'd shove them down his throat myself.

"Ready to go?" Oskar was already out of the hospital bed and wearing a pair of jeans. His arm was in a sling, but his chest was still bare.

"Yes. I guess I'm on nurse duty. No dirty jokes please."

"Come on. You've got to give me a pass today." He put his arm around my neck and leaned on me more heavily than I expected.

"I plan on putting you in the bed as soon as we reach your room and then we can watch something on TV until you fall asleep. I know you think you're being Mr. Tough Guy with the no-pain-meds thing, but once the stuff they already gave you wears off, you're going to be cranky and exhausted."

Surprisingly he didn't argue, allowing me to lead him back to his bedroom with no additional comments or jokes. Once he was in the bed, he let out a little sigh of relief, and I felt bad for him. Obviously, he'd underestimated just how much energy walking back to his room would take. Poor guy.

"Can I get you anything? Are you hungry? Or maybe you need some water?" I twisted my hands as Oskar resettled himself on the bed, yanking the covers up almost to his chin.

"Now that you mention it, I do need something." His voice was so soft it was almost a whisper. I leaned closer to hear.

"Whoa!" I shrieked when Oskar suddenly grabbed my hand and tugged me down on top of him.

"That's what I needed. I feel better already." Oskar smirked when I pushed up on one elbow and glared at him.

"I was actually worried, you jerk."

"Baby, I'm fine. This isn't my first time at the wrong end of a gun."

"Not helping."

He was quiet for a minute and then sighed. "Seriously, this is all I need. Having you here and knowing you're safe is all I need in this life."

It was so unexpectedly sweet that it was a real struggle to hang on to any anger toward him. How did he do that? In the span of a moment, the man could have my emotions ricochet between annoyance and adoration. And I wasn't sure what to think about that.

Or what to do about the fact that my heart was no longer my own.

CHAPTER TEN

Hailey

The next few days were spent with me trying to keep Oskar from overexerting himself and Oskar trying to convince me to play naughty nurse games with him. The man was truly the worst patient in the world, but after the scare of hearing he'd been shot, I was willing to put up with almost anything if it meant he was safe.

I could get used to this, I thought when I woke one morning to the sight of Oskar's face. It made me smile. After everything we'd shared, I felt closer to him than ever. Being unexpectedly married to a man I hadn't seen in years was definitely not a part of my five-year plan, but

I couldn't regret it.

Maybe there was something to being spontaneous and going with the flow. Priya was always telling me to take life as it came and roll with things more. Usually just the thought of proceeding without a color-coded itinerary made me feel like I was going to break out in hives, but this was just... right. Being with Oskar came naturally as if this was the way things should have always been. I'd been away from work for a few days, and nothing had fallen apart. The world hadn't stop spinning at all.

Just then Oskar grunted, and his eyes opened. It happened so quickly that I had no time to look away or pretend to still be asleep, so he caught me pushed up on one arm and staring at him like a stalker.

"Good morning. Was I snoring?" He blinked several times before wiping one large hand over his face self-consciously. "Or drooling?"

"No. You're adorable."

He grimaced. "I am not adorable. But I guess that means I was relatively well-behaved while we slept."

I smiled contentedly when his arm tightened around my

back and yanked me closer. "This is probably a mistake, but how does one misbehave while asleep?"

He snorted. "Are you kidding? This is me we're talking about. I expected to wake up jerking off with one hand and grabbing your boob with the other."

I pinched him in the side, and his deep rumbling laugh echoed throughout the room. There was very little light coming in from the window, so I wasn't sure what time it was. More importantly, I didn't really care.

"It's still early. Maybe we have time to get some breakfast before you have to go in to work."

At the mention of the word *work*, I pulled the covers over my head. Getting out of bed meant facing the very real problems waiting for us. It wasn't so bad to want to avoid all that a little longer, right? Here in this room, Oskar was my husband, I was his wife, and all that mattered was how we felt when we were together. But we'd been locked away ignoring the world for the better part of a week. I had to get back to my usual routine even though I wasn't looking forward to it.

As soon as we left we'd have to deal with my family, his job, and the threat against me. So I snuggled closer and buried my face in his chest.

Don't judge me.

Oskar chuckled and then peeled back the comforter slightly until he could see my eyes. "Is someone tempted to play hooky for the first time ever?"

"It's not the first time I've played hooky."

"Calling ahead to say that you'll be out of the office isn't playing hooky. That's a scheduled leave of absence. When have you ever just not shown up?"

"It's happened."

At his incredulous look, I rolled my eyes. "Okay maybe it hasn't. But I really don't want to go in."

His eyes softened. "I get it. But I am supposed to be the voice of reason and remind you that life has to go on. We can't just hide out here forever. But if it helps any, I'm not thrilled about letting you out of my sight either. Maybe I should just keep you here forever."

The dirty look in his eyes almost made me want to agree. But he had a point. If I start avoiding work for various reasons, then whoever shot at me had gotten the upper hand. I wouldn't be made a prisoner by fear.

"You're right," I said finally.

"As usual," Oskar finished.

I glared at him before my eyes landed on the white bandage around his arm. "How are you feeling? Any pain?"

He shrugged. "It sucks. I'll get over it. Noah will put me on light duty today."

"What? You shouldn't be working. You got shot!"

"It probably won't be the last time, butterfly." He kissed me square on the mouth before getting out of bed, leaving me staring at his back.

I was still wearing the oversized shirt I always slept in, so I quickly pulled on a pair of yoga pants. Oskar pulled on a pair of jeans and managed to get a big sweatshirt over his head with only one arm pulled through.

When he saw me looking, his lips quirked. "It'll do long enough for us to have coffee. I just want to spend a little time with you before you have to leave. Plus, I want to find out who'll be assigned to you this morning so I can put the fear of God into them. They'd better be on their A-game if they're going to protect my wife."

I was hit with an overwhelming rush of affection. Obviously, we hadn't been back together long, but there was a tiny part of me that was starting to believe this might actually work out. We just worked together. Oskar's devil-may-care personality was the perfect counterbalance to my slightly uptight, control-freak side. He was ridiculous sometimes, sure, but he always made me laugh and didn't seem to mind my quirks at all. He was so easy-going that he just took everything I did in stride.

And he hadn't mentioned anything about getting a divorce again.

Coffee was followed by an awkward shower where I tried to wash him without getting the bandage wet and Oskar spent the entire time trying to grab my ass. By the time we were done, half my hair was wet, which meant it was about to frizz up big time and I would definitely be late.

Totally worth it by the way.

Oskar left me to get dressed alone, and by the time I made it downstairs, I was wearing a pinstriped black skirt paired with a festive pink blouse. My hair was slicked up into a massive bun, and I'd gone with more dramatic makeup than usual. When you don't feel your best, a cute outfit and makeup always helped.

Oskar raised his eyebrows and I could tell he wanted to

makc a sexy comment and was only holding back because of the woman standing next him.

"Hailey, this is Gemma. She's going to escort you to work today."

My face must have shown my surprise because Oskar raised an eyebrow. "Weren't expecting a female body-guard, huh? I'll have you know that we have two on staff. The other one, Diana, is just on pre-maternity leave."

"What's pre-maternity leave?" I asked.

Gemma rolled her eyes. "It's when your extremely overprotective husband interferes with you doing your job or pretty much anything just because you're preg-nant. We're lucky Rafe doesn't carry her everywhere, too."

Oskar chuckled. "Anyway, Gemma is a total badass and can even knock me on my ass. Even more impressive, she's married to Matthias and that's about as scary as it gets."

She shoved him aside. "I'm going to tell him you said that."

"You don't need to do that," Oskar added quickly.

I stood on tiptoe and pressed a kiss against his cheek. "Be careful today."

He cupped my chin. "Always. I'll see you tonight."

We both watched as he walked out. Then Gemma turned to me. "Is there anything you need before we leave?"

"A time machine. So I can go back to this morning. Oskar makes it really hard to get out of bed." Once I realized what I'd just muttered I blushed, but luckily Gemma didn't seem to mind.

"I hear that. I could have used more cuddle time myself this morning, but Matthias had to go."

She looked so bummed that I was intrigued. Matthias was perfectly polite every time I'd interacted with him but honestly... the guy was pretty scary. He was leaner than all the other guys, but there was just something in his eyes that made me think he'd seen some bad stuff. Probably done even worse stuff.

But here was Gemma looking dreamy-eyed about the guy, so maybe she could help me out. Who better to ask for advice than someone who was married and was clearly happy?

"This is a nosy question."

Gemma smiled knowingly. "My favorite kind."

"How do you make it work with one of these guys? They're so intense and they do scary stuff all day. I mean, Oskar got shot and acted like it was just another day at the office. I have no idea what I'm doing. Is it stupid to think we could have something here? Something real?"

"It's not stupid at all. The man is clearly head over heels about you. It's a little weird actually. He's never serious about anything, and then he looks at you and it's like, BAM."

Her description made me laugh. "That's how I feel too. But how do we make things work after all the danger and excitement is over. What's the secret?"

Gemma started walking and I fell in step next to her as we headed to the elevator. "The secret is the same as how to do well with anything in life. Practice. You'll fight. Then you'll make up. Then you'll fight again. But every time, you'll learn how to exist better together."

Exist better together? I guessed we'd have to see about that.

Oskar

After I knew Hailey was taken care of, I went to see Noah for my assignment. I'd already taken some painkillers to take the edge off my throbbing arm so I knew light duty was a good idea, but that didn't mean I wanted to be stuck in the office doing paperwork. Noah knew how I felt about being sidelined. I had way too much energy to be caged.

"There you are. I was about to come find you."

"Why?" I looked between Noah and Jonas who was sitting in the chair in front of his desk.

"Because, Jonas is going to question some of Evan's gambling buddies. I figured you might want to ride along."

"Oh, thank god. I figured you'd come up with some bullshit assignment to give me something to do."

Jonas got up and clapped me on the back. "Everything you do is bullshit."

"Whatever, man. As long as I'm not filling out paperwork, I don't care what you say."

I followed Jonas down to the garage level. Gemma's car was gone, and I wondered how things had gone with Hailey's drop-off. Calling and asking would probably be a little much, but I couldn't deny that I was worried. Not being fit to protect her made me twitchy.

"Your girl is fine," Jonas drawled once we were in the car and pulling out into traffic.

"How did—"

"You've got the look. All of us have worn it at some point or another. When JJ had her stalker, you don't think I was tempted to follow her ass every minute of every day?"

It shouldn't have made me feel better, but it did. Caring this much for one person was unfamiliar territory, and I couldn't ignore the nagging feeling that we were all missing something important. Maybe it was just because I was cranky and in pain, but I wanted to figure out what the hell was going on. Then I could finally believe that Hailey and I would be okay.

"So, tell me about these guys."

Jonas shrugged. "Typical bookies from my research. I'm not expecting much, but maybe they can at least tell us how long this has been going on. If some of his debt has come due recently, or if they put pressure on him, it could be motive. He needs cash quick, so he comes up with this kidnapping scheme."

"For Hailey's sake, I hope he's not the guy. She's had enough family drama already."

It took a minute to find parking, but when we walked into the apartment building, I had to do a double take. The kind of gambling that a man like Evan Livingston would be doing didn't take place in a low-income building. Jonas saw my expression and shrugged. There was no elevator, so we walked up three flights.

"It's this one," Jonas said, tilting his head toward unit 3A.

He knocked, and a few seconds later the door was opened by a guy who was even bigger than me. Light reflected off his bald head and highlighted the scowl on his face.

"Mr. Hoss is expecting you." He moved aside so we could enter.

As we passed, his eyes scanned over us both as if

assessing our weaknesses. I was glad I hadn't worn the sling and instead just opted for a button up shirt and jacket to conceal the bulky bandage on my arm. This guy looked like the type to go right for the wound if we ended up in a fight.

"Gentlemen, what can I do for you?" A middle-aged man with thinning brown hair and a belly hanging over his belt got up from the leather couch in the middle of the room.

The apartment was small but now that we were inside, I could see signs of wealth. The furniture was all leather and looked to be good quality. A massive flat screen hung on the wall, and there was artwork everywhere you looked. He followed my gaze and smirked.

"The neighborhood might not be the best, but people here know how to mind their own fucking business."

"Right. We're here to talk about Evan Livingston. He owes you, right?"

Hoss chuckled and then dissolved into a wet, hacking cough. "That little shit? Yeah, he owes me. Big time. You here to pay his debt or something?"

I glanced over at Jonas before interjecting. "Wait, why

would he need someone else to pay his debt? The guy is rich enough."

We had our own theories about why Evan couldn't get the money from his father, but I doubted he'd tell his bookie that he wasn't good for it.

"He's not that rich anymore. At least that's what I heard. But I'm not one to gossip."

Jonas rolled his eyes. "How much does he owe you?"

"Millions. But that's not anything new. He does this every few years, gets on the hook for millions and then finds some way to squeeze the money out of his old man." He let out another hacking cough. "That dude does some wild shit when he gets desperate. Maybe he'll kidnap a family member again and get the money that way."

Next to me, Jonas stiffened. Suddenly it felt like all the air in the room was gone, and I couldn't breathe. A hot bloom of rage started rising from my gut.

"What does that mean? *Again?*" I asked, trying and failing to keep from shouting.

Hoss smirked. "So that's what it is? I figured you two were cops or something. But you must be here about the girl."

Jonas pulled out his wallet and threw a wad of cash on the table between us. "Tell us what you know."

"I don't know much. But people talk, you know? Evan got in trouble a few years back. Owed the wrong people, if you know what I mean. So he arranged for someone to kidnap his sister, thinking that he could ransom her back and their father would pay without knowing that she was never really in any danger. Only it didn't go down quite like that, and the kidnappers wanted more."

"They tried to hurt her?" Jonas asked.

"Livingston security at the time caught the guys before they could get their hands on her. Once the truth came out, Elijah Livingston paid off the debt and hushed the whole thing up. But people around here have long memories."

"So do I," I muttered before glancing over at Jonas. He needed to wrap this interview up so we could go have a little chat with Evan.

And by chat, I meant my fist in his face.

CHAPTER ELEVEN

Oskar

By the time we reached the Livingston building, my rage had multiplied exponentially. All I could think of was what Hailey was going to feel when she found out her whole damn family was lying to her. Again.

Jonas clapped me on the back. "Are you okay to do this?"

"Yeah, I'm fine. It's just, she deserves better than this, you know?"

He nodded solemnly. When we entered the office, the security guy waved us through. They were so used to us being here for Hailey that they didn't even question our presence anymore.

We took the elevator to the top floor and then took a left and marched down to Elijah's office. His assistant tried to stop us, but I barged right in, shoving the door open so hard it crashed against the wall.

Elijah was on the phone, and he whipped around when the door opened. "What the hell is going on?"

Jonas stood in front of the door and crossed his arms. He looked dapper as always in his perfectly tailored slacks and a silk shirt that fit like a second skin. That guy loved clothes more than I did, but somehow, he still looked completely badass.

"Elijah, we need to talk."

"You need to get the hell out of my office."

"I would be happy to, except we have a little problem. You neglected to mention the extent of Evan's gambling debts. We thought it was a recent problem. Only for the last six months to a year. But apparently, it's been a problem much longer than that and has been going on for years. Something you neglected to tell us."

Elijah inhaled deeply, popping out his chest. "My family business is none of yours."

"Except it is. Hailey believed in her brother because well, she loves him. God knows why. But you neglected to mention he owes that kind of money, and he'd do just about anything to get it, wouldn't he?"

"I'm calling Blake. You're off the case."

"Try it. Hailey wants me on the case. And let's be real, I'd do this for free." I rolled my shoulders and made an effort not to wince. Stupid arm still hurt.

That's because you were shot less than a week ago.

Yeah, whatever.

"Were you planning to mention at any point that Evan tried to organize the kidnapping of his own sister for ransom money once before?" Jonas's question carried even more intensity because of the quiet way he delivered it.

Elijah blanched. His dark skin went slightly ashen before he swallowed roughly. "I'm calling security."

"Do what you want, but we're getting some goddamn answers today."

"You have no right. This is a family matter."

"Maybe it *was* a family matter, but that was before someone started taking shots at my wife."

Elijah slammed his hand on the table. "She is *not* your wife."

"Well, funny thing is there's this little piece of paper, you know, all legal-like that says she is, so you just have to get used to it. In the meantime, I'm trying to figure out who's trying to kill her, and you keep threatening me at every chance you get."

"This is my family I am trying to protect."

I shook my head. "We're not getting anything out of him, Jonas."

Jonas was studying Elijah. "I have to tell you Mr. Livingston, that is an excellent blazer. But honestly, with those pants, don't you think the shirt clashes a little bit with the charcoal? It's doing too much."

Oh my God. "Do we have time for this?"

Jonas shrugged. "I'm just trying to help the man out. You would think since he's your father in law you'd want to help him too."

"Shut up. Let's go. If he's not going to tell us the truth, we have no choice but to go to Evan." And that guy was a slippery fuck. But I honestly did believe he wanted to help his sister. We'd just have to figure out what the hell was going on.

***

Hailey

I could practically feel the whispers all around me. Everyone had heard about my little tiff with Dad, which was fine. They could say whatever the hell they wanted. I didn't care. *Except, you do care.*

Okay fine, I do care. But there was nothing I could do about it, and I still had a job to do. Jasmine still needed a full marketing roll out plan. I had Miles Everson, Head of the Marketing Department in my office when my mother showed up.

Miles slid a furtive glance between us. "Listen Miles, why don't you give us a few. I'll come down to you when I'm done."

He looked more than thrilled to have made his escape.

"Mom! Hi. I didn't know you were in the office today. Did we have plans for lunch and I forgot?"

My mother shook her head. "No. I actually came to see your father." The casual way that she said that told me she still didn't know that I knew the truth about her adopting me. And as I watched her, I realized I'd felt it my whole life, the distance she put between us. Maybe it was a distance that *she* felt. She must have tried, after all, she took in someone else's daughter. But that certainly couldn't have helped with her drinking problem.

"I haven't talked to Dad all day, so I don't know what he has planned."

My mother slid into the chair opposite me. "Uh, that man. Well, I guess I will just have to go to the restaurant and have a drink while I wait."

Just that statement alone made me gnash my teeth together, and before I could recall the words, they were tumbling out. "Seriously? Why do you do this?"

"I don't know what you mean, love."

"This, the happy lush. You've been to rehab, Mom. You would think that you would take that recovery seriously."

"Well, I tried to tell you at the time I didn't need rehab."

"I beg to differ, Mom. When you're incapable of performing your daily tasks, and showing up for your appointments, yeah, you have a drinking problem. Remember, we went to therapy. Was I the only one there?"

"You make too much of this."

The frustration was almost too much to bear. "Mom, do you realize that I am killing myself with this perfume because of you? I just want you – well, I want you to see that I'm trying."

"Yes, the perfume is fine. It's nice, okay? I swear, you're the one who needs therapy with all this 'Mom, just love me' business."

"Oh, so we're doing this now?" The words tumbled out before I could even stop them. "You know what? My whole life, I have been begging you to love me, to pay attention, to see that I was doing my best, but it was never good enough. Even now, as I try to make things just right for you, you can't even care because all you're thinking about is your next drink. We've all tried. Me, Dad, Evan. We're exhausted."

"Don't you dare tell me about being tired after what your father has put me through."

"Mom, I know what he put you through. I mean, the fact that he forced you to raise someone else's child, yeah, I know."

Her eyes went wide, and her mouth fell open. "You know?"

"Yeah, I know. It's why Dad and I are currently not on speaking terms."

"Oh, then why are you concerned about me not loving you?"

"Maybe you do love me in your own way. After all, you did agree to raise me. But you've always acted like you resented it."

"What I resented was your father having an affair and then attempting to blame me and my drinking. What I resented was having his love child foisted upon me."

"Then why did you do it? Why did you take care of me? You didn't have to."

She thinned her lips then. "I did my duty. You were just a little girl. I tried to love you the best that I could."

"And I appreciate it. I just—I don't know. I wish things could be different. I wish you would get help Mom."

"Yes, well, I wish your father had paid more attention to me over the years, but he didn't. So we all can't have what we want."

I couldn't help myself. "I'm sorry he did that to you. It's not fair. I wish I'd known."

She sniffed. "Anyway, I did go to see your father, but there were two men in there, and they were shouting. Security was on their way."

"Security?"

"Yes, a male, quite large. One blond guy. Looks like a Viking. I've seen him here guarding you."

Oh God, Oskar. What was he doing here? And why hadn't he called me? What were the two of them fighting about this time?

"Well, anyway, I wanted to tell you that the perfume was nice."

"Nice?"

"You did a good job. I do love you, Hailey."

"Mom, I—" I didn't know what to say. Hell, I didn't even know if I still should call her Mom after everything I discovered last week. "Thank you."

She looked like she wanted to say something else but honestly, I didn't know how to talk to her at that point.

"Well, I'm going to go see your father. Maybe he's done with those men."

"Yeah. Maybe." As I watched my mother, I eased into my chair, emotions running through me. What in the world had just happened? All my life, I'd wanted her approval. I wanted her to tell me I did a good job. I'd wanted her to love me. But somehow when she said the words, I had no idea what to do with it.

CHAPTER TWELVE

Oskar

Jonas took a cab back to headquarters, while I went to check on Evan. If he didn't tell me the truth, I'd have to drag his ass back to the penthouse. When I stepped out of the elevator, Dylan was taking the trash out. "The piece of shit had you taking out his trash?"

"If I thought I could trust him, I'd make him do it himself. But I don't trust him not to try and shove himself down the trash shoot, so I'm doing it."

I shook my head. "Sorry kid."

"Yeah, whatever. Am I still grounded?"

"Yeah, for the time being, but it might be easier to move this party to the penthouse. Some new stuff has come to light."

Dylan rolled his shoulders. "As long as I can stop watching reruns of Bravo, I'll be happy."

I groaned. "Ugh! He's watching Bravo?"

"Oh yeah, my life is a *Real Housewives* episode right now."

"All right, come on. We might as well take him and get something to eat."

"Yes, thank God. A couple of days with him and you'd be better off to shoot yourself in the eyeball. Yeah, I've gotten to watch sports, but it's been a challenge keeping him from *betting* on them. You didn't say I had to hold on to his laptop, so every time I turn around, they guy is basically dumping money down the drain."

I rolled my eyes. "Son of a bitch."

"Yeah, tell me about it."

I found Evan furiously typing on his phone. When he

saw me walk in, he tossed the phone down quickly. "Oskar. Is Hailey okay? What are you doing here?"

I was warmed by the fact that he asked about Hailey first, but that didn't mean I trusted the fucker. "Get your jacket, we're getting something to eat."

"Oh, thank God. You finally realized I've been telling the truth?"

I shook my head. "I wouldn't go that far. You've told pieces of the truth, but you left a whole swath of things out, so you and I and Dylan are going to have a long chat about it over food. And if you lie or make shit up again, I swear to God I'm going to admit you to holding at the penthouse. That means you'd get three squares, but there's no TV. We were doing you a service by letting you stay at home. But if you lie again, no more."

Evan shifted on his feet and shoved his hands on his pockets. "Okay, yeah, I'll tell you everything."

I grabbed him by the shirt collar and pulled him close. I wasn't actually going to hit him, but I figured I could scare him a little bit. I'd feel better because the kid was a little fucking liar. "You fuck with me again, and Hailey is not going to be mad when I hurt you. Do you understand?"

He nodded frantically.

"Get your shit."

Thirty minutes later, we walked into a noodle place six blocks south. We'd still driven because, why ask for trouble? Once we sat down I started grilling him. "So, do you want to explain about the time when you tried to have your sister kidnapped?"

He slunk down on his seat. "Fuck. I was 18. I didn't know what the fuck I was doing. I was probably high all the time."

"You tried to have your sister kidnapped."

"But it didn't happen. I just needed my Dad to pay the ransom. He was threatening to cut me off if I didn't get off the drugs and the booze and stuff, and I was dumb. That was so stupid. I never should have done that."

"Yeah, no shit, Sherlock, but you did. So, we're going to talk about why you did that, who you called, and all those details, because it makes me less inclined to believe that you're not behind this whole trying-to-kill-her situation."

"I thought we covered this. Did you check the ballistics

on the bullets? They had to be from a different gun because I didn't even fire mine."

He was right about that. Well, at least the 'not firing his gun' part. Matthias had checked the thing over. It never fired. And it had a broken pin. It wouldn't have fired anyway, so he definitely wasn't the shooter.

"Look, I've done some fucked up shit. I have. But I swear, I wouldn't hurt her. She's my baby sister. All I ever wanted to do was protect her or have her leave me alone. Yeah, she was annoying, and I hated that Dad always took her side and wanted to protect her, but I also hated that Mom treated her like shit, you know? So I was caught between trying to protect her and being jealous of her. I wouldn't actually have hurt her. And even that guy that I paid to try and kidnap her, honestly, he was just going to keep her in his apartment for two days until Dad paid the ransom. Easy as that. Then I was going to be the one to deliver it. I had a whole plan. It was stupid, and of course, I got caught. But never once was I going to hurt her."

"You know, what's weird? I don't see any record of this in police reports."

"Are you crazy? Dad buried it. The police were never

called. The FBI was never involved. He had some private security guy working for him at that time. Basically, a fixer type of asshole I guess, the same one that probably got the adoption set up, but he made it go away as if it never happened, and Hailey never knew."

"Yeah, you're damn right she didn't know, because she'd have you strung up by your toes."

"I keep telling you, she knows I would never want her actually hurt."

"Then you need to stop acting like it."

"Look, I know it looks suspicious. I do. I just—" He sighed. "I'm a fuckup."

I threw my hands up and leaned back in the seat. "Yeah, no shit."

Dylan snorted at that. "Sorry man, but you *are* a fuckup."

"I know it. I've been a fuckup my whole life. But I'm trying. I am."

He shifted uncomfortably in his seat, and I narrowed my gaze at him. "What? What's going on?"

"I have to use the head."

I rolled my eyes. "Kid, take him."

Dylan groaned and glowered at me, but he stood.

"Get up. Let's go."

The bathroom was in my line of sight, so I could easily keep an eye on them.

The two of them went in, and I momentarily breathed a sigh of relief. I checked my phone and sent a text to Noah, letting him know where I was and what was up. And then I sent a text to Hailey, letting her know that I'd be home a little bit later. Hell. It wasn't something I'd really given much thought to before. When Noah had offered me a job and a way out of my old life, I'd thought it would be a temporary situation. Somehow, years later, I was still working for him, and honestly, there was nowhere else I'd rather be. I checked my watch and frowned. Where the hell were they?

When they finally came back out, Dylan came out first and checked the hallway, and then turned left. But when Evan came out, he checked the darkened hallway and then bolted right. Something in my eyes must have telegraphed a 'what the fuck' to Dylan because he spun around and sprinted.

"Shit." I slid out of the booth and headed for the front door, intending to double back toward the alley.

After nearly bowling over a family with small children, one of whom tried to climb me like a tree, I sprang out the front door and hooked right. I turned just in time to see Dylan deliver an elbow straight to Evan's face. Evan went down like a bag of rocks.

But then Dylan was fighting someone else. Hands up, feet in boxer stance, constantly moving, ducking, and weaving. Jab. Jab. Hook. Uppercut. Knees, oh solid. Ugh, lots of knees. Another quick punch, another grab, one more knee for good measure. And then, whoever it was that they'd encountered in the alley was down, not moving.

I ran up to them. "Oh shit. You didn't leave any for me."

Dylan was barely breathing hard. "Well next time, old man, don't take so fucking long."

"Oh, really? What the fuck? I'm only twenty-six."

"And yet somehow, you don't actually get out here quick enough."

"I went to the front to cut him off."

From the ground, Evan moaned.

"Jesus Christ, pick him up. Put him in the car. We'll take him back to the penthouse. I'm tired of this shit." I decided when we got back to the penthouse, I was going to make him talk, one way or another.

Hailey

I wished I'd gotten all the information I needed all at once. Like some big family intervention.

Hey, baby, by the way, you're adopted. Your father had an affair, and I've been resentful ever since. Oh, and hey, Evan found out about you too. And he's also resentful. He blames you for everything.

That would have stripped the Band-Aid off.

I felt bad for Diana, who'd been the one to drive me back from work. Aside from asking her how she was doing, I'd pretty much ignored her.

When we arrived back at the penthouse, there was a commotion happening. There were some guys in the conference room, and Jonas was among them. I looked around for Oskar, but I didn't see him. He'd mentioned being on light duty, so he should have been around, right? Unless something had happened.

I was almost to the kitchen, when I heard the elevator again, followed by the sound of someone groaning. I backtracked and peered around the corner. That's when I saw my husband.

I knew it was silly, but I still got a little rush every time I said the word to myself. He was my husband.

He hasn't told you he loves you.

And yeah, we needed to get to that. Granted he hadn't brought up getting divorced again, so that was probably a good thing.

Evan was behind Oskar with Dylan bringing up the rear. "Hey, Evan, are you okay?"

My brother didn't meet my gaze. "Yeah, I'm fine." When I got a good look at him, I saw his lip was bloody and his nose looked crooked.

I glared at Oskar. "What happened?"

My husband just shrugged. "Don't look at me. That was the kid, who by the way, is a total badass."

Dylan shifted on his feet sheepishly. "Look, sorry to disappoint you, but he was kind of getting in the way of my real fight. I had to put him down so he'd be out of the way and not get himself hurt."

Evan gingerly touched his nose. "Nice job getting me out of the way."

Oskar jumped in. "Well, next time don't try to run."

"Yeah well, some guys I owe money to had just walked in to the restaurant, so I figured it was probably best if I made myself scarce."

I put my hands on my hips. "Evan?"

My brother just shrugged. "Yeah, I know. I'm a fuckup." He turned his attention to Dylan. "So, do you guys have a doctor who can fix my face?"

Dylan groaned. "Fine, come here. I'll put you in the medical bay. We'll call the doc to come and set your nose."

"Is he good? Because I'm too pretty to trust my face to just anyone." Evan chuckled at his own joke and then winced and put a tentative finger to his nose.

Oskar smirked. "Don't worry, we have Doctor Frankenstein on retainer."

Honestly, I could slap my husband sometimes. "Do you want to explain to me what is going on right now?"

"Someone tried to take him. I don't think it was anyone he owed money to. As far as I could tell, those guys were still in the restaurant. No one followed me out the front door, and no one followed them, which means that someone was waiting outside for him."

"See? I tried to tell you. He didn't try to hurt me."

"I know. But there are some other things that you need to know about Evan, sweetheart."

"I get the feeling I'm not going to like this."

"You're not. But you need to know, and I refuse to hide anything from you anymore."

He wrapped his arms around me and I sank into his hold. I never wanted to let him go. "You know what? Right now, I just want to hold you. It's been a hell of a day, and in case you haven't heard, my husband got shot earlier this week, so I just want to hold him for a minute and not think about anything bad. So, can this wait?"

I could feel his breath hitch in his chest where my cheek

was pressed, but then he exhaled slowly, and his muscles relaxed. "Yeah, this will keep."

"Okay. Now, if you don't mind, just hold me for a minute."

"Yup, that I can do."

CHAPTER THIRTEEN

Oskar

I stepped off the elevator and went directly to the kitchen. Breaking the news to Hailey about what her piece-of-shit brother had once done wasn't going to be easy. Hell, I needed a drink first.

When I turned the corner, I stopped short when I saw Hailey sitting at the counter in the kitchen talking to Evan. Rage bubbled right beneath the surface. That fucker had the nerve to sit there next to his sister, shooting the breeze as if he hadn't once gambled with her life like it was a game of high-stakes poker.

My breaths were coming so fast I felt lightheaded.

Hailey smiled, and it only made it worse. Because she was so trusting, yet this whole time, the Judas in her world was the man she'd assumed meant her no harm.

If I hadn't been interrupted right then, Evan would have undoubtedly ended up in an ambulance, but just as I stepped forward a hand clamped down on my shoulder. I glanced over to see who had a death wish. Anyone who would touch me when I looked like I was ready for battle deserved what they got.

"Not now, Matthias."

"You're going to want to see this, mate. I've got something."

It was on the tip of my tongue to tell him to fuck off when his words finally penetrated.

"Got something?"

He glanced around. "I got a facial recognition hit on the shooter."

I reared back. "The shooter? But I thought..."

The hand that was still clamped on my shoulder tightened briefly. "You're not the only one. But it turns out that we were looking in the wrong direction this whole time."

Intrigued, I followed him to his room after giving Evan and Hailey one last look. She was safe from him here surrounded by our guys. Which made me feel better but still didn't stop the urge to go pound his face a few times just as payback for his past transgressions.

Matthias's room was slightly bigger than everyone else's, probably to accommodate all the computer shit he needed to do his tech magic. The dude had a gift with computers and kept Blake Security and our clients safe from any cyber security threats. He had a particular knack for working his way into government systems and getting access to all kinds of information that no one was supposed to know about.

I wasn't going to ask exactly how he'd ID'd the shooter because the answer would probably entail a bunch of stuff he couldn't admit to anyway. Plus, it didn't really matter. He'd come through and that was all I needed to know. The exhaustion of being on edge for the past few weeks was starting to catch up with me. This was my job and I was used to the stress involved when protecting a client, but it was entirely different when you were protecting someone you loved.

Matthias threw himself down into his desk chair, and his fingers flew over the keyboard. Almost instantly, he brought an image up on the screen and then zoomed in. I peered closer.

"Look familiar?"

I shook my head. Matthias was staring at me in a way that was unnerving. The dude was always dialed to intensity level one thousand, but there was something different about the way he was looking at me. It was almost... accusatory?

"What the hell is going on, Matthias? Am I supposed to know who that is?"

He sighed. "Is there anything you want to tell me, mate?" His accent was always thicker when he was annoyed, and right then he sounded like he'd just jumped the pond.

"Don't do that. You know me. I don't bullshit. If I tell you I don't know the guy, I'm not yanking your chain."

Matthias hit a few other keys and brought up another image. "He works for a mob boss that operates mainly out of Eastern Europe. They call him Mr. X. Recognize him?"

It used to always sound so cheesy when people would say that their world stopped spinning. But I finally understood the expression because in that moment, I was so stunned I almost fell over. It had been so long since I'd heard that name that it sounded foreign to hear it spoken out loud. Maybe in some ways Mr. X had become a part of my past that I'd buried so well I'd managed to convince myself it had never happened. I was good at fooling myself, apparently, because I'd legitimately never thought I'd hear the name again.

"The past is never really buried, is it?" I whispered.

"Believe me, I know. I've been there." Matthias wasn't known for being the most compassionate guy on the team, but in that moment I could see true understanding in his gaze.

"Mr. X was a client way back in the day. That was handled years ago. Noah made sure the whole organization fell apart. He was in jail." The tone of my voice must have clued Matthias in that I was unraveling because he leaped to his feet and pushed me down into his seat.

"Take a deep breath. I don't need your big ass falling over in my room, because I'm not giving you CPR."

I sat there, listening as Matthias called someone, the

words not registering. All I could think of was that last day when I'd seen Mr. X and known that things had to change. It had been a defining moment for me, the final nail in a coffin that had been partially closed for years. Most people don't survive long in the underworld unless they already have no soul. I had felt mine slowly slipping away until I met Hailey. She'd reminded me of what was good and right in the world, and I'd known that I wanted more than money and a life on the run. And even though I'd had to leave her behind, she'd been the catalyst and driving force behind everything I'd done since to build an honest life for myself.

"Noah and the others are waiting in the conference room."

I follow him blindly as we walk out of his room and down the hall. When we passed the kitchen, I glanced around for Hailey but the room was empty.

"She's with Lucia." Matthias answered the question before I could ask.

Noah was already in the conference room when we arrived, along with Rafe, Jonas and Dylan. Tyse walked in behind us and took the chair right next to the door.

"Okay, let's get started. Ryan is out with a client, but I'll brief him when he gets back." Noah looked over at Matthias, who stood and walked to the laptop set up at the front of the room.

"This is Mr. X." He pulled up the same image he'd shown me.

Noah sat up straight and then glanced over at me. "Are you serious?"

Matthias chuckled darkly. "Some of you have heard of him. He's a major European mob boss who was in jail until recently. We're still not sure how he got out, but his network is completely intact and seems to have thrived while he was incarcerated."

Noah grunted. "What I want to know is how this could go down without anyone telling me?"

Jonas leaned closer. "I get the distinct feeling that wasn't an accident. Someone didn't want you catching wind of this until it was done."

"Government?" Noah looked annoyed. "You know what that means."

Matthias shrugged. "That was my first thought. There's no way ORUS isn't involved somehow. Any time the government has some shady business they want handled, ORUS gets it done. There's no way Ian didn't know."

The silence that settled over the group made my stomach twist into knots. Even though I had never been a part of the shadowy, secret organization that had trained most of the others, I knew plenty about how they operated by now.

And if they were involved, then this Mr. X sighting didn't bode well for any of us.

Hailey

I looked up in alarm when the door to Lucia's room burst open and calmed only marginally when Noah came through.

"Babe, you just scared the crap out of us!" Lucia held a hand to her throat before leaning up to offer her cheek for a kiss.

Noah obliged, bussing a quick kiss against her cheek. "Sorry, Lu. I wasn't thinking."

Oskar appeared in the doorway behind him. If I had to

pinpoint exactly what was wrong, I probably would have said his eyes were off, but I knew for sure was that *something* was wrong. Oskar looked like he'd aged about ten years overnight, the lines around his eyes standing out in stark relief against the bluish shadows under his eyes. I stood slowly, my legs stiff after being curled up on the bed while I chatted with Lucia. After talking to Evan earlier, I'd been a little bored and lonely when he'd had to go with Ryan to meet our father at work. Evan had been resistant to having bodyguards following him everywhere, but now I think he could see that it was turning out for the best. With constant babysitters, he couldn't get himself into any trouble. It was forcing him to be responsible the way he should have been all along. Evan had seemed more settled and serious than I'd ever seen him.

It was a hard thing to acknowledge, but my big brother really had been weak and easily influenced by others. For so many years I'd looked up to him and loved him, the way little sisters everywhere did. But I'd had to accept that my brother had some pretty major flaws and I couldn't help him fix those. He had to want to fix them himself. It seemed like he was finally taking some responsibility and working to be better.

"I'll see you later, Lucia. We can finish binge watching the rest of *Grey's Anatomy* later."

She nodded. "Right. I'm not letting you out of it. I still can't believe you hadn't seen it before. Everyone needs McDreamy in their lives."

Chuckling, I waved before stepping out of the room and closing the door behind me. Noah had a hard time keeping his hands off his wife on any given day, so I figured I'd save anyone else from getting an eyeful they weren't ready for.

Oskar pulled me into his arms and rested his head on top of mine.

"Hey, is everything okay?"

He squeezed me tighter. "Come with me. We need to talk."

I followed him, not letting go of his hand the whole time. Maybe if I held on hard enough it would keep me steady through whatever was coming. Seriously, when had good news ever followed the words "we need to talk". Clearly something had happened, and it was going to be something I wouldn't like.

In his room, Oskar closed the door behind us. When he tried to lead me over to the bed, I dug in my heels.

"Just tell me. What's happened? Another threat?"

He sighed. "Not exactly. We've got some leads but not enough, and it's difficult to judge whether you're safe here. I'm researching some alternate safe houses for you."

The things he was saying made sense, but there was definitely something that he *wasn't* saying.

"Safe houses for me. Where are you thinking we should go?"

He didn't answer.

"Oskar, you'd be with me in the new safe house, right?"

When he wouldn't meet my eyes, I yanked at his hand. "No way. You're not sending me off somewhere without you."

He looked at me, and I shivered at the empty look in his eyes. Oskar was always joking around with me and saying inappropriate things. It was chilling to look into his eyes and see a stranger. It was like he'd walled himself off from me already, as if we were already separated in spirit.

"Butterfly, I think it's for the best if Rafe or Matthias takes you away somewhere. With their skills, I know that you'd be safe."

Horrified, I snatched my hand away. It would have been bad enough if it were just a suggestion, but he was talking as if it was a done deal. For all I knew, he'd already packed my clothes and was planning to stick me in an unmarked sedan right after dinner.

"No way." I didn't look at him again as I walked to the door and yanked it open. "Noah! Rafe! Whoever else is here!"

Something crashed behind me, but I didn't look back as I charged down the hallway. I could hear doors opening and closing upstairs and then the sound of feet on the stairs. Matthias poked his head out of his room when I passed.

"You too!" I yelled as I passed by. "Everybody needs to hear this."

JJ looked up from the magazine in her hands when I stormed into the family room. "Damn girl, you're on the warpath. What the hell did He-Man do now?"

I felt a little silly now that I'd brought everyone down

here for this, but that wasn't going to stop me. "Oskar just told me that he's going to send me away. I'm not okay with that."

Oskar's shoulders sagged. "It's not safe for you to be around me. The others can protect you while we figure out how to draw the heat off me. Your brother will remain under our protection, but there are so many other factors to consider. This needs to be done. It's the only way that I can keep you safe."

I shook my head. "I don't agree with that. How is putting you in danger instead of me supposed to be any better? Don't you get it? If something bad happens to you, then I might as well have died anyway."

Everyone went quiet. Oskar stepped closer. "I can't take any chances here Hailey. This is way things need to be."

"So, you think you can just make decisions for me? Screw that. That is *not* how things are going to be with us. I'm your wife, and that means that I'm with you all the way. Even when things are bad. Even when things are scary. Just try and get rid of me, mister, and you'll be getting a swift kick in the balls!"

The guys all exploded into laughter, and my face flamed. Even though I'd called them all downstairs, in the midst of my rage I'd totally forgotten we weren't alone. I squared my shoulders. I wasn't going to be ashamed. Nothing that I'd said was anything less than the truth, and if embarrassing myself in front of everyone got my point across, that was a loss I was willing to take.

"She's perfect for you, mate. Don't fuck it up." Matthias's voice carried over the sound of the group's laughter.

Oskar was chuckling too. I wasn't sure if that was a good thing or if I needed to make good on my threat. Then he completely swept my legs from under me with two simple sentences.

"Yes, she is. That's why I love her."

I clasped my hands together to keep from reaching out for him. Ever since the day I'd said I love you and he hadn't said it back, I'd told myself that it didn't matter. That his actions meant more than any phrase ever could. Oskar showed me how he felt about me in tangible ways, the things he did for my comfort, the way he worried over my safety. All of that was potent and real evidence of how he felt, and I'd come to accept that.

But hearing it out loud had an impact I hadn't expected. Tears pricked at my eyelids, but I sniffed, refusing to let them fall.

"You love me?"

He grinned. "Of course I do. How could I not? You're my ballsy, mouthy butterfly. What the hell would I do without you?"

"I don't know, but I don't plan to find out. Because I love you too, and you're not getting rid of me."

Amid a chorus of whoops and cheers, Oskar scooped me up and tossed me over his shoulder. I pinched his back and then huffed when I couldn't find even an ounce of fat.

"Put me down, you Neanderthal!"

He squeezed my legs. "Not a chance. I need to get you alone so we can have a rational conversation. Preferably naked."

CHAPTER FOURTEEN

Hailey

He loved me. He'd blurted it out to everyone. Why hadn't he said anything before? After the first time I'd said it, I'd assumed he didn't feel the same. I'd stopped hoping to hear it, thinking that Oskar just wasn't ready to go there yet, but he'd made it clear tonight that he was all the way in.

He carried me easily toward our room, a hand on my ass. The sound of his feet on the carpet told me that we were in the upstairs hall. Any second now, we would be inside. And then he would be inside of me, and I wouldn't feel so empty.

He loved me, and we'd wasted so much time. For once I wasn't alone. Never mind my emotional outburst in front of everyone. I wouldn't judge myself too harshly because... he loved me, and I was about to have an orgasm. *Several* of them.

Multiple orgasms awaited me, and I couldn't wait.

Oskar fumbled with the door. Finally, he adjusted his hold on me long enough to get it open. Once inside, he pushed the door shut and then eased me off his shoulder. But instead of sliding me all the way down, he pressed me against the door.

"You love me."

I nodded with a smile. "Yep. You love me too."

"Duh."

He kissed me hard then, his lips crushing mine. His big body pressed me against the door as his tongue slid in and out of my mouth, branding me.

With me braced against the door, his hands shifted and slid up under my top, cupping my breasts, kneading them, rolling his thumbs over me nipples.

Jesus. A cry tore out of my lips and I rocked my hips into him, inviting him to go exactly where I wanted him to be.

With a muttered curse, I fumbled with his belt buckle, and reached between our bodies to help him. Closer. I just needed to be closer to him. A naked him. Right the hell now. *Jesus*— I needed him inside me. Batting away his hands, I used my dexterity to remove his belt and unsnap the top of his jeans.

"Seems like you've had some practice with that, butterfly."

"Please shut up and fuck me."

His laugh cracked through the silence. "Your wish is my command."

With a series of wiggles, we were able to get his jeans past his hips. Then his boxers. He reached under my skirt and hooked his thumb inside my thong before making a fist.

I pulled back and met his gaze, all the heat and intensity of it, boring into my soul. And then he flicked his wrist and the thong snapped in two as if it were merely a rubber band.

Yes. Hell yes. Before I knew it, the smooth head of his cock nudged my entrance.

"Hailey." His voice was part growl, part question, all Oskar.

"Yes, I need you."

He nudged his length against my center and I moaned deep. All I needed was him. Him inside me, making me shake, making me want nothing else. That's what I needed. Later we'd do all the feelings talk. *Much* later. "Oskar, now, please."

"You haven't come yet," he muttered.

Oh, my big, beautiful Viking. Always so worried about me.

"Do you feel how wet I am? I just need you inside me, now."

The growl was a low rumble. "Jesus, fuck, Hailey. Condom."

"I'm on the pill. Oskar, just—"

With a muttered curse, he slid the head of his cock inside, and all the way home. "Shit," he muttered through clenched teeth. "So fucking good."

I groaned. Holy hell. Against the door, Oskar slowly loved me, rocking his hips in and out. Pulling out until just the tip of him grazed my slick entrance, and then kissing me softly, slowly deepening the kiss as he slid all the way back in, stretching me wide, making my head roll back.

His fingers intertwined with mine over my head, and he placed a hand on my ass for extra support.

It didn't take long. I felt my body going tight. I knew what was coming. Welcomed it. Welcomed that quiet ownership. I needed this. A few weeks with him had ruined me for anyone else, ever again. Good thing he loved me.

He picked up his pace. "Come for me. I need to feel you—"

He didn't have to tell me twice. I threw my head back and screamed his name, breaking apart as he loved me.

He cursed low and tightened his grip on my ass. His hips picked up the pace, faster and faster, taking me deep, taking me high. And then, when my orgasm rolled into a second one, threatening to break me apart, I whispered, "I'm never letting you go."

"Good, because I plan on keeping you."

I dropped my head forward and bit into his shoulder. Going limp, I knew that I was going to keep him forever. I didn't believe in fate, but I knew I was right where I belonged.

CHAPTER FIFTEEN

Oskar

"So, is this what life is usually like around here? Hanging out, watching movies, and teasing each other?"

Hailey snuggled closer, pulling one of the million throw blankets Lucia insisted on leaving around over her lap. We were currently in the family room waiting for JJ to get back with the popcorn. I would have to remember to thank both JJ and Lucia later. They'd gone out of their way to be welcoming to Hailey and make her feel like a part of the group.

When I'd decided to bring her to the penthouse, I'd only

been thinking about her physical safety. But after more time with her, I could see how isolated Hailey was from everyone else around her. She spent most of her time working. Even though she worked with her family, they focused on business and didn't seem to concern themselves with what Hailey liked to do outside of work. Did anyone ask her if she had hobbies or interests separate from her family's perfume empire? It didn't seem that way. But in the past weeks with me, she'd opened up in so many ways. Her eyes seemed brighter and she wasn't so stressed. It was an unexpected gift that I'd been able to give her. Friends who didn't give a shit about how much money she had or could make.

Oblivious to my thoughts, Hailey took another noisy sip from her slushy drink. Something she'd never had before but I'd insisted was an important part of the movie experience.

"I'm starting to think this whole bodyguard thing is just a cover. You guys probably don't do anything most of the time."

I snickered. "Except that one time I got in the way of a bullet, right?"

Her eyes were twinkling when she raised one eyebrow.

"Did you? I seem to remember you getting a scratch or something." She squealed when my fingers dug into her sides.

"Okay, okay. I guess I have to give you that one. Especially since you scared the hell out of me. But I'm happy to see that your everyday life is pretty normal. It makes me feel a little better."

Although she'd been pretty cool about the danger inherent in my job, I knew it bothered her. The truth had come through in some of the little things she'd said and the questions she'd asked. I got it. We were at the beginning of building something real, and I would be worried about her if the tables were turned. But after telling her about all of the training and precautions we took, she seemed okay with it.

It was going to take me a while before I completely adjusted to the idea of letting Hailey all the way in. But I had agreed to stop trying to shield her from the ugly parts of my past, and she had agreed to cut me some slack on my overprotective tendencies. It wasn't perfect, but we were making it work.

I had to give her credit. She had adjusted to my life a lot better than I'd expected. Maybe I could relax a little now. As long as nothing crazy happened, she'd be okay. I was lucky that Rafe or Noah hadn't gone on any of their intense side jobs lately. The last thing I needed was Hailey catching a peep at how beat up those fuckers looked after a rough night.

Hailey leaned over to reach for her wineglass but paused with her hand outstretched. Her eyes were caught on something across the room. Her mouth fell open. "Oh my god."

I looked over to see what had caught her attention. Gemma stood in the doorway to the room with a black eye and a huge bruise on her arm. The black pants and shirt she wore were relatively unscathed except for the slight rip in one of the sleeves. I was scared to look at her shoes.

"Family movie night? Sweet." She waved at everyone. "I'll join in a few. I just need to clean up."

Oh shit. This was exactly the kind of thing that Hailey had been worried about. She'd already told me that every time I left, she was scared I'd get hurt again. Now she was staring at a woman she was coming to know as a friend who looked like she'd been a victim of domestic violence.

I watched Hailey warily, unsure of how she'd react. It wasn't as if she didn't know that Gemma worked as a bodyguard also. Part of me wanted to list off the many deadly skills Gemma possessed, but before I could do that, Hailey took a deep breath.

"Do you need an ice pack? I can get one for you."

Gemma smiled. "Thanks, but I've got it. I'll ice down after I take a shower." She turned to Ryan, who looked slightly green. "Good work tonight."

Ryan blinked. "This shit is not normal." The other man wasn't nearly as roughed up as Gemma, but he had a long scratch on one cheek and looked like he'd just seen a ghost.

I understood how he felt. He hadn't been on the job that long, and all of us had moments when things got a little too intense. This job was about being strong mentally as well as physically.

I patted Hailey on the arm. "I'll be back in a minute. I just need to talk to Ryan."

She nodded knowingly. "He looks like he could use a friend. And maybe some tequila."

"I'll keep that in mind." As I was walking out, JJ passed by holding two large bowls of popcorn. "Save me some!"

She snorted. "You snooze you lose, big boy!"

Ryan was in the kitchen staring into the refrigerator like it held the secrets to the universe. Without turning around, he asked, "Are you here to give me a pep talk?"

"Nah. I'm not really the pep-talk type. This is more like advice that you should hang in there, because I know shit looks wild right now."

"Wild doesn't even begin to cover it. Gemma was... man, I would have never thought one small girl could move like that. She just ..." He made a few karate moves. "Hell, I don't know what she did, but she took out like three guys before I even knew what was happening. How is Matthias okay with his wife being in that kind of danger?"

"First, don't let any of the women hear you say that shit. Are you trying to get all of our asses kicked?"

He sat at the counter. "I know Gemma was ORUS, but I don't think I really understood what that meant before."

"There are a lot of things in play you don't understand

yet. The people Noah, Rafe and Matthias used to work for aren't the type you ask questions about. Trust me."

Ryan shrugged. "Trust hasn't worked out so well in the past. Trust gets you killed."

"You trust Noah, right?"

"Yeah, I do."

"Good. Because it's all going to make sense eventually."

When I turned, Noah was standing behind me. "Thanks, O, but I've got it from here. Come with me, Ryan. I have something to show you."

I watched them go before going back into the family room. Ours was an unconventional family, but that's exactly what we were, a *family*. If things went south, protecting Hailey was all I cared about. Having a literal band of former assassins on your side was pretty decent when it came right down to it. And I was grateful to have their support when it mattered most.

***

Hailey

I was laughing at something JJ had just said when Oskar came back in. Gemma had changed clothes and was curled up on the other couch with Matthias. JJ was sitting in her husband's lap in the armchair. It was the weirdest collection of people I'd ever hung out with, but somehow it made sense. Everyone there respected everyone else. No one was made to feel different or like they weren't good enough.

It was strange to finally find acceptance amongst a group that I'd known for such a short time, but I'd never felt this comfortable around anyone but Priya. Definitely not with the private school crowd that I'd been with from grade school until graduation. In our circles, appearances were everything. Who you were friends with, what designers you wore, and what car you drove were all more important than whether you were smart or kind or compassionate.

But here, everyone was so different but respected nonetheless. There were so many different personality types represented but they all had their place. And I had my place.

With Oskar.

It felt like we were settling in. Maybe if Oskar hadn't

been forced to leave three years ago, this is where we would have been all along. The thought made me smile. It was almost like time restoring things back to where they should have been.

Ever since I was a little girl, I'd always hated the concept of fate. It made me feel like nothing I did really mattered since things would go where they wanted to anyway. But now, I had a different perspective. It wasn't that my actions didn't matter but rather that my mistakes wouldn't derail what was meant to be. Oskar and I were meant to be.

And now we were together once more. Nothing that had happened three years ago had changed our destination. It was comforting to think that nothing going forward would ever really pull us apart either. We'd always find our way back to each other somehow. Like magnets.

"You've been quiet," Oskar commented when he sat back down next to me.

JJ glanced over. "She's probably not used to all these people blabbing at once. You'll get used to it. That one never shuts up." She pointed at Oskar.

"Jonas, can you muzzle your girl?"

We all laughed as JJ threw a handful of popcorn at him.

"Okay let's get this movie started before these two kill each other." Jonas picked up the remote and started the movie, some superhero film I hadn't even heard about.

Oskar bent low. "We don't have to stay. I know this isn't your thing."

"It's not that. I've just been thinking. You know, about what happens after this. After all the danger has passed and things go back to normal."

His smile was gentler than I'd ever seen on him before. "What happens is we do normal things. Go out for pizza. Make out in movie theaters. I love you every day. And you love me right back."

Even though my heart was busy melting at his sweet words, my brain refused to turn off. I had seen what happened when couples got together quickly. Often their relationship couldn't hold up under everyday stress. All of the decisions that were part of making a life together were easy to ignore at first but then practicality would rear its ugly head.

Clearly, we wouldn't live here in the Blake Security headquarters forever. Would it be strange to have Oskar move into my penthouse? Or would that offend him and make him feel like a 'kept man'? Maybe he'd rather we live somewhere that was chosen and paid for by both of us. But that seemed silly when I had so much wealth. It was a touchy subject, but we couldn't ignore the differences in our financial status. Would Oskar feel demeaned if I paid for certain things?

It was a lot to think about.

When I looked over at him, his eyes softened. "Your brain never takes a night off, does it? I know it's hard, but I don't want you to worry. It's all going to work out."

I wanted to believe him. So much. But there were so many things that we hadn't learned about each other yet and all of them had the potential to torpedo our marriage. It started off wrong but that didn't mean I wasn't completely committed. Oskar was my husband and I wanted to do whatever was necessary to make it work.

"We're in this together. Forever."

Maybe there was something to that whole fake it 'til you make it thing. Because just saying the words really did make me feel better.

CHAPTER SIXTEEN

Oskar

The rest of the night, I focused on relaxing with Hailey and enjoying some rare time off. She enjoyed pointing out all of the inconsistencies in the film, and I enjoyed trying to feel her up under the throw blanket.

It hadn't slipped my mind that there was one huge thing hanging over us. Evan. I still hadn't told her about her brother's attempt to kidnap her years ago. Matthias's new intel about Mr. X had become the focus of the investigation, but that didn't mean that we could afford to ignore Evan's history. Even though he wasn't responsible for the shooting at the gala, it didn't mean that he was completely innocent.

If I'd learned anything over the course of my life, it was that you couldn't afford to ignore any potential enemies. Evan might not have tried to hurt Hailey this time, but he was still a liability to our future. She deserved to know what the men in her life had kept from her. I shook my head. Elijah Livingston played the part of a concerned father well, but his actions betrayed that there was a lot more going on under the surface, and I didn't trust him either.

Hailey squeezed my hand, pulling me out of my thoughts.

"You look so deep in thought. Are you still mad about me asking why Superman couldn't be in this movie?"

I chuckled. "At this point, I'm pretty sure you're just trolling me."

"What? I don't get it. Superman would have saved the day from the beginning."

Matthias walked by, not bothering to conceal his smirk. "Good luck with the DC vs. Marvel conversation, mate."

When I turned back to Hailey and saw her grin, I

laughed. "Okay, you are trolling. I refuse to listen to any more of this blasphemy."

Hailey followed me back to our room. "Are you sure? I was thinking we could have a little role-play. You can be Thor and I'll be Black Widow."

I grabbed her hand and pulled her inside, shutting the door behind us.

Hailey backed up to the bed slowly, teasingly lifting the edge of her shirt. "I figured that would get your attention."

As hard as it was to put the brakes on when she was about to fulfill one of my favorite fantasies, I held up a hand.

"Wait, Hailey there is something that I need to tell you. I meant to earlier, but then I got pulled into a meeting with Matthias."

Hearing the intensity of my voice, she dropped her shirt. "And I thought we'd gotten past all the bad news."

"Not quite."

She sighed and sat on the edge of the bed. I wasn't sure if

that was an invitation for me to join her or if she'd prefer space, so I remained standing.

"I went with Jonas to question one of Evan's bookies."

Her head snapped up at that. She crossed and uncrossed her arms before dropping her head into her hands. "Okay, wow. I mean, I know you guys said he had a gambling problem, but it's just really hitting me that Evan was out there making deals with shady people. It doesn't seem real."

"Unfortunately, it's very real. He was in pretty deep to some scary people."

She shook her head. "What the hell is wrong with him? He could have gotten himself killed!"

Unable to stand being across the room from her any longer, I walked over and knelt at her feet. "He could have gotten you killed, actually. The guy we talked to said Evan has gotten in trouble before. That time, he attempted to have someone kidnap you thinking he could extort ransom money from your father."

All the color drained from her face, and I regretted my blunt words. Telling her all at once had seemed kinder, like ripping off a bandage, but Hailey just looked so betrayed.

"I'm so sorry, butterfly. But I thought you had a right to know."

Her fingers tightened on the covers, twisting the fabric. She nodded quickly but wouldn't look at me. I put a finger under her chin and lifted until she met my gaze. Tears glimmered in her eyes.

"Am I really so disposable to everyone in my life?" she whispered.

I pulled her into my arms and she collapsed against my chest, her shoulders shaking with silent sobs. From her perspective, I could see how it would seem everyone in her world had betrayed her at some point. She'd spent her life trying to gain her mother's approval only to learn the woman wasn't her mother and had been forced to accept her. Her father cared mainly about his business and Hailey's talents that could make him money. Her brother resented her and considered her a block to gaining his inheritance and a bargaining chip with his debtors.

Who could blame her for feeling lost and alone? Everyone that she'd trusted had let her down at some point, including me. I had let her down, too. Which was something I'd have to live with forever.

But that was never happening again. I vowed that from that moment on, Hailey would know she had one person in her corner who would always put her first and fight to the death to keep her safe. Her husband.

Me.

"I'm sorry, butterfly, but he's never going to hurt you again. I'll make sure of that. I know this is a lot to take in, and I shouldn't have just dropped that on you."

Hailey wiped her eyes as she sat back. I didn't really want to let her go yet, but in this I would follow her lead. She'd had enough of her choices taken away by people who were supposed to love her.

"It's not your fault. Does it really matter how you say it? Finding out your own brother once tried to have you kidnapped isn't the kind of thing that you can sugarcoat."

"Maybe not, but that doesn't mean it's easy to hear either. And that's not even the whole story."

She waves her hand. "Wait, there's something worse? What could be worse than being almost kidnapped by your own brother?"

Fuck my mouth. In that moment I hated every instinct I'd had to be honest. Seriously, I could have been playing hide the hammer right now but oh no, I'd wanted to tell her the whole truth. Having scruples was pretty damn inconvenient sometimes.

"It's about your father, Hailey."

Hailey

Oskar was watching me like he thought I'd break down again at any moment. Not that I blamed him. The poor guy was just the messenger and kept having the unfortunate task of telling me about my dumpster fire of a family.

I sighed. "You might as well just tell me."

The arm around my shoulders tightened. Oskar looked like he'd rather be anywhere than sitting on a bed with me delivering bad news. I had to give the guy a break. He'd actually been willing to turn down sexy time in order to tell me the truth. There had to be a gold star in his future just for that.

"Your father knew about Evan's plans. His security team at the time got wind of the threat before it happened."

I shrugged. "Okay, so he protected me. He figured out that I was in danger and kept me safe. That sounds like something he would do." Some of the tension that had gathered in my stomach settled slightly. Oskar had made me think it was something really bad. But it made total sense that my father had taken care of a threat behind the scenes without letting me know. But when I saw Oskar's face, I realized that wasn't what he'd meant at all.

"That's not what you meant, was it?"

"No. Actually... I meant that he knew it was Evan. He found out that your brother was behind it and... he covered it all up."

"Right. Of course. What else could you have meant? It's not like you'd expect normal decency out of anyone in my family."

He squeezed my hand. "I just thought that you deserved to have all of the information. I'd want to know."

I thought about it. Maybe I wasn't that evolved because there was a part of me that didn't want to know about any of this stuff. For years, I'd lived blissfully unaware.

How did it help me to drudge all this stuff up now? I could have gone to my grave never knowing how weak and opportunistic my father and brother really were.

"I don't want to talk about this anymore."

Oskar nodded quickly and looked around the room as if it would give him a clue about what to do next. "Sure. Let's talk about something else. Anything else."

We sat there in silence for almost a full minute before I burst out laughing. For a while, he just watched me with a small smile. The kind you use when talking to someone you aren't sure is entirely sane. But eventually his lips stretched into a big grin, and then a chuckle slipped out.

"I'm glad you can see the humor in all of this," he managed to get out between breaths.

"Reality is truly stranger than fiction. I couldn't even make this stuff up!"

After our laughing jag passed, we ended up tangled together on the bed, limbs intertwined, my head settled on his chest. Below my ear his heart beat a rhythm that sounded like comfort. Like home.

"I'm glad it was you," I whispered finally.

He raised his head so he could see me. "What was that?"

"This whole thing sucks, but I'm glad you're the one who told me. If I have to hear bad news, it helps to hear it from someone who loves me."

"I do. I really do. Which is why I hate hurting you."

"Are we crazy for trying to make this work?"

When he looked at me, I gestured between us. "You don't have a great experience with family, and clearly, neither do I. Are we setting ourselves up for failure here?"

Oskar leaned back and I followed, curling up on the bed next to him. Right there, it seemed a lot easier to breathe, like all the problems surrounding us were outside and couldn't reach us. It was an illusion, but just then I was happy to take all the help I could get.

"Hailey, things are different with us. We're not the same as your parents or your fucked-up brother."

My eyes were closed when I answered. The events of the night were catching up with me, and it hit me all at once just how tired I was. "Why?"

"Because we're honest with each other even when it

hurts. We aren't doomed to repeat our families' mistakes. We're making our own choices. And we choose to stick together."

"Promise?" I whispered.

I don't remember hearing his response, but my heart knew.

CHAPTER SEVENTEEN

Oskar

When I looked down, Hailey's eyes were closed. Her long inky lashes rested on her cheeks, creating little shadows. She looked so peaceful that I hated to move her.

Fuck it. I wasn't going to. We could sleep right here. I dozed off with Hailey plastered to my front and one hand moving up and down her back gently.

The next thing I knew, I was waking up to someone moving on top of me. I groaned. Hailey had moved so she was straddling me, and her hips were working against mine, rolling in little circles. I glanced around, noting the lights were still on since I hadn't gotten up to cut them off before I'd conked out. It was disorienting as hell to wake up like that, but I wouldn't have changed it for the world. If my wife wanted to grind on me in her sleep, who was I to complain?

"Hailey? Are you awake?" I whispered.

I wasn't sure if she was even aware of what she was doing. She was a touchy little thing in her sleep. I don't think she even knew how many ways she'd wrapped herself around me at night, but usually it wasn't quite this blatant.

"Oh no, I'm totally asleep." Hailey pushed up on her hands and winked at me. Her hair fell around her face in a dark cloud of kinky curls. Some of her eye makeup had run, so she had little black circles beneath each eye.

She still looked like a fucking goddess.

"You're killing me, butterfly." My hands flew up to grasp her hips, trying to slow her movements. There was only so much I could take, and if she kept gyrating against me the way she was, I was going to come in my pants like a kid.

"No, I definitely don't want to do that." Hailey leaned forward, trails of her hair falling over me like a curtain.

I shivered. The strands left a ticklish sensation behind that made me feel like I was hyper sensitive to touch. Maybe it was just the shock of waking up while halfway to an orgasm, or maybe it was just Hailey. But every single thing seemed to feel better, and every inch of me was finely tuned to each move she made.

"Make me forget, Oskar. Touch me and make me forget everything except us."

Someone else would probably have a better way to handle that but I had no idea. I'd already decided that Hailey could have anything she wanted of me anytime. If what she wanted was my body, then that was check... and check.

My fingers took their time tracing the delicate line of her collarbone. At another time, maybe I would have gone straight for the good stuff but I wanted to treasure her, every part of her. Hailey sucked in a deep breath, her breasts rising and falling with the motion as my fingers took a walking tour past her neck and up to the curve of her ear. She giggled when I traced the line of her ear and then across her cheek and over her lips.

"You are truly a miracle, you know that?"

Her eyes popped open at my words, and I could see the vulnerability that she never showed anyone else.

"I wish I felt that way."

"Well if you don't feel it, then I'll have to tell you. Every day."

Her hands covered mine and trapped them against her stomach. "I'd rather you showed me."

The raspy tone of her voice let me know playtime was over. Her dark eyes glowed with promise and purpose as she leaned down to kiss me.

Desire exploded between us as soon as our lips met, and all of the restraint I'd been holding on to by a thread unraveled. Hailey let out a soft hum of satisfaction when I flipped us over, using the weight of my body to keep her still. The way we fit together was magic, and I stopped trying to be so controlled for once and just let myself go. With her, I didn't have to be any one thing. I could just be whatever I was feeling in the moment, and she was with me.

Totally with me, I thought as her hips undulated beneath mine. Fuck, she was perfect.

She must have been feeling the same urgency because her hands tugged and pulled at the sweatpants riding low on my hips like she was about to tear them off. I leaned back just enough to slide them down and could kick them off. Her eyes sparked once I was naked, which made me flex instinctively. It was such a turn on to watch how she responded to me, how crazy she could get when she wanted me. Even though it still wasn't half as wild as I felt every time she even looked at me.

"This is what I needed." Hailey purred as her hands coasted over every inch of my bare chest and then skimmed appreciatively over the abs I worked so hard on in the gym. She glanced up at me and then bit her lip before her hand circled my cock.

My head fell back at the intense pleasure of her warm hand working over me. "I need to be inside you, butterfly. You drive me so crazy."

"Wait, but I wanted a chance to play a little." Hailey squeezed me teasingly, her eyes lighting up at my groan.

"Play all you want."

She pushed me back on the bed and stretched out next to me. In this position she had plenty of room to work and took total advantage of it. Her curious fingers danced over every part of my chest, even dipping into my belly button. Her lips followed, turning each touch from a tickle to a white-hot burn. By the time she got below the belt, I already felt like I was on fire.

"You always take such good care of me. I want to take care of you, too." Hailey's breath washed over the head of my dick, and I clenched, trying not to buck my hips.

She didn't have a ton of experience, and the last thing I wanted was to scare her off. A monster dick to the eye was enough to traumatize women who were used to performing the act.

Then her lips closed around the tip and I lost it.

My hips jerked again forcing my length deeper. But she didn't seem to mind, just grasped the base with her other hand and hummed approvingly. The vibration set me off, and I had to grab the headboard behind me because it felt like I was flying. The edges of my vision blurred, and stars danced above us as my wife proceeded to blow my mind and my cock off.

Hailey stayed with me, making the sexiest little moaning sounds as she swallowed, and I swear I didn't know it was possible to be this turned on. The pleasure rolled over me in waves, going on and on until I felt wrung out.

"Jesus, Hailey." It was all I could say when I finally regained the ability to speak.

Meanwhile my wife was licking me leisurely, like a little cat who'd been satisfied with a treat. She stretched sinuously before wrapping herself around me again.

"Mmm, hearing you got me all worked up." She lifted one leg over my waist and I could feel how wet she was against my leg.

"You like teasing me, don't you?" I shifted until she was resting on her belly and I was behind her. That gave me the perfect position to play with her a little and also punish her for taunting me with her sexy little body.

"It's not my fault you're so easy." Hailey's voice broke when my hands landed on her hips. I took my time squeezing and molding her lush bottom. Then I leaned over and gently nipped her with my teeth .

"Oh!" Her little yelp of surprise was so genuine that I had to laugh.

"Didn't expect that, did you?"

The coy look she sent over her shoulder proved she was enjoying it just as much as I was. Then her eyes almost rolled into the back of her head when I thrust deep.

Immediately she clamped down on me, and I paused, trying to keep control even while it felt like her internal muscles were strangling me. I came down over her back, until she was blanketed in me, my hands landing on the bed next to where hers were buried in the sheets.

We panted together as she rocked her hips back, catching my rhythm. Every time, we moved together like we were two halves of a whole, and too soon I was balancing on the edge of a monumental orgasm. Hailey's hands came over mine, her fingers clutching at mine helplessly as we raced toward the finish line together.

"Oskar, please."

The desperation in her voice made me feel just as needy. I wanted her to be right on that edge with me, ready to fall off together. Balancing on one hand, I used my other to stroke her clit, grinning in victory when she cried out and shuddered beneath me. Unable to hold back anymore, I stopped trying and let myself ride that wave right beside her.

Exhausted, we collapsed on top of the sheets, our legs and arms tangling together. For a long time we just rested there, the only sound between us our labored breathing and the rustle of the sheets between our legs as we moved. Hailey rolled over and put a slightly damp hand on my cheek. Her forehead glistened with sweat, and several dark curls were stuck there. Her breathing had finally slowed down, but her eyes were still closed. Masculine pride made my chest swell. Yeah, I'd tired her out.

I loved her so much. Fifty years from that moment, I hoped we'd still be just like this. Wrinkles and all.

"Marry me, butterfly. For real this time."

Hailey

My eyes popped open. Oskar was smiling at me with this tender look in his eye, the one that always made me feel completely loved. As if he wanted to make sure I got his meaning, he grabbed my left hand and kissed my ring finger.

"You're my wife and I want everyone to know."

He suddenly jumped up and scrambled to his feet. Alarmed, I scooted back until my back hit the headboard. "What are you doing?"

"Hold on. Just wait. I need to do this properly."

He started moving around the room, opening drawers and looking under random books. I had no idea what he was looking for, but I didn't want to interrupt him. Watching him move around while he was still naked was truly a sight to behold. I bit my thumb watching his muscular backside as he walked, and I pressed my thighs together.

Good lord, it had to be criminal for a man to look that good. Shouldn't I have been used to how insanely fine he was by then? But somehow the effect never seemed to wear off.

Oskar caught me watching him and paused. "Stop looking at me like that. You know what that does to me."

I slid down in the bed but then peeked out from behind my hands. "Maybe you should come back over here and make me."

He groaned. "You're not going to distract me. I have to do this right and proper. Ah, here it is."

When he came back to bed, he was holding something in his hand, but I couldn't see what it was.

"The past three years, I've been so focused on building a

new life that I don't think I realized how empty it all was. I was alive, but I wasn't living. Then you came back into my life. It was like seeing the sun again after being underground. You make me better. You make everything better. And selfishly, I don't want to go back to living in my cave alone."

Stunned, I watched as he dropped to one knee beside me. "Oh, Oskar."

He swallowed several times before continuing, like he was nervous. The sight melted me almost as much as seeing him get down on one knee. This sweet, gentle giant was nervous about pouring out his heart to me? It proved the drunk Vegas Hailey actually had better taste than the serious, staid Hailey I tried to be the rest of the time. Because none of the other men I'd dated had treated me like this. Like being with me was so special that they were nervous about messing it up. Oskar treated me like my love was a gift.

It was a lot easier to trust your heart to a guy who treated it like it was a precious jewel.

"I left you to save you, but really, you're the one who saved me. So, Hailey Livingston, I need to ask you to save me one more time. Will you marry me? Again?"

Emotion clogged my throat until I was almost unable to speak. Finally, I managed to squeak out, "This is doing it right and proper? With a candy ring?"

Oskar glanced down at the obnoxiously large red candy ring in his hand. "You're just as sweet."

"So are you," I whispered. "And I would love to marry you. Again. Forever."

CHAPTER EIGHTEEN

Hailey

If you'd asked me just a few months ago to describe my dream wedding, I would have been able to paint you a picture. Big white dress, lots of flowers and everyone I know in attendance. I wouldn't have mentioned walking toward a groom that I was already married to while wearing whatever off the rack dress was available.

I wouldn't have mentioned being so happy that I felt like I was overflowing with it.

Maybe everything happened the way it did to prove how little all that stuff mattered. Because suddenly, when I thought of a dream wedding, the only thing that stood out in my mind was the man I'm walking toward. A couture dress would have been nice but not necessary. It would have been great to have all my friends and family there, but I knew I could get by without that if I had to.

As long as I was walking toward Oskar, then all of those other things were just details.

"Are you sure you don't need me to stick around? I can ask Noah to reassign me?" Oskar had been so sweet all morning, not leaving my side except to get food and brush his teeth. Truthfully, I'd been basking in the attention, absorbing the incredible feeling of being the center of his awareness.

But I would never want his worry about me to stop him from doing his job. He was so supportive of my career, and I wanted to be that same kind of cheerleader for him. His work was important to him, and he kept other people safe, which was very noble. I would never get in the way of that.

"No, I'm okay. You go be all badass. I'll see you tonight."

He hesitated briefly before kissing me on the nose, and then he followed Jonas down the hallway that led to the conference rooms. He'd already warned me that they had some strategy meeting that was certain to take all morning but then he'd have the afternoon free.

Lucia and JJ entered the kitchen then chattering away about something. The only words I could make out were *bowl of dicks*. It was funny that when I'd first gotten here, their blunt style of speaking had made me a little uncomfortable, but I'd become totally used to it.

"Do I even want to know what a bowl of dicks is about?" I asked before taking the orange juice out of the refrigerator.

JJ tilted her head to the side, seriously considering the question. Lucia rolled her eyes.

"You know better than to ask that kind of question by now. We don't need to give her any encouragement. She's already consistently pissed off at the world."

"Not the world," JJ promised. "Just Jonas. He has a knack for annoying me. Luckily after I tell him to eat a bowl of dicks, he more than makes up for it by *giving* me good dick. So there is that."

"I think we all do just fine in that department." Lucia glanced over at me and pursed her lips. "Speaking of... you guys retired early last night."

I could feel the blood rushing to my face. "We were tired."

JJ chuckled. "Leave her alone, Lu. Like you and Noah haven't ducked out early plenty of times to get it on. Wait, what is that?"

I glanced up to see JJ gaping at me. "What?"

Moving way faster than I'd expected, she darted forward and grabbed my left hand. She held it up to see the candy ring on my third finger. Her mouth fell open.

Lucia pushed her out of the way. "I have a feeling this is about more than you having a craving for strawberry candy."

I grinned. "It is. Oskar asked me to marry him last night. Again. For real this time with all of our people there."

Lucia held her hand over her heart. "Awww. He's such a softie! I'm not surprised because the way that man looks at you is just... whew!"

"He looks at her like she tastes like a candy. And he's a sugar addict," JJ interjected.

"Well, he's addicted to Hailey," Lucia said matter-of-factly. "This is so exciting! Tell me everything! What did he say? I can't believe he didn't say anything to us. I'm so good at romantic surprises, I could have helped!"

JJ picked up my hand gently and examined the candy ring. "This puts new meaning to put a ring on it. It's so silly it's actually genius. Who knew he could be romantic? I guess he isn't all talk."

"He's definitely not all talk," I mumbled. I ignored their knowing smiles. "Anyway, I know we haven't known each other that long but you guys have known Oskar for a long time. Will you help me plan a small wedding? I really want us to have one that we actually remember."

Lucia squealed with delight. "We get to plan a wedding? Yes! Don't worry about a thing. We've got this. And my grandmother can even do the cake. Nonna has a bit of a soft spot for Oskar. Well, she likes anyone who loves to eat."

I hugged them both. "Thank you. You don't know how much I appreciate it. Because I have no idea what I'm doing, and I want this to be special. Things are crappy with my family right now so I need something good to look forward to."

Lucia put an arm around my shoulders. "We understand about family drama. One day when we have more time,

I'll tell you the story about how I thought my brother was dead for ages."

I blinked at her and then shook my head. "Okay, you win. Family drama sounds like an understatement in that case."

Lucia grinned. "It's complicated. It always is around here. But we get things done."

JJ had already pulled out her phone. "We have so many contacts in the fashion world. Despite what people think, fashion assistants are the ones who truly run the world. We can probably get you a bunch of dresses and accessories lined up pretty fast. How quickly are we talking?"

I thought about everything that Oskar and I had already been through. Tomorrow was never promised and if I had my way, I'd marry him that night. I wasn't giving him the chance to get away from me again.

"Yesterday."

JJ put the phone to her ear. "We're going to need to call in reinforcements."

"Who are you calling?" Lucia asked.

"Gemma and Diana. We need everyone's help if we're going to pull off an overnight wedding!"

Oskar

As the meeting wound to an end, Noah shuffled the stack of papers in front of him. He had been less than pleased when Jonas reported on our conversation with Evan's bookie, and I figured he would be having his own conversation with Elijah soon. It was better if it came from him.

Hailey's father already hated me, and it wasn't like I could blame him. I did marry his daughter in secret, abandon her for years, and then proceeded to debauch her every chance I could. What could I say? I loved every minute of helping Hailey discover her naughty side.

But it's probably not something my new father in-law will forgive me for anytime soon.

"Next item on the agenda is congratulations. To Oskar." Noah's grin was so wide I was surprised I couldn't see his tonsils. Which meant that Hailey must have told the girls about my proposal.

Either that or they'd caught sight of the ridiculously big candy ring on her finger. It was campy and crazy and exactly the kind of thing that we'd one day tell our kids about. It hit me right then just how much I was looking forward to all of that. The possibilities of an entire future with Hailey. How the hell had I gotten so lucky?

"Thank you. I just hope that I can make her happy before she figures out she can do much better than me."

Jonas clapped me on the back. "Excellent news, man. Hailey is perfect for you. I wish you guys all the happiness in the world."

I glanced over at Rafe, who was smirking from across the conference table. "Come on. Hit me with it. After all the shit I've given you over the years, I'm sure you've got something to say. No ball and chain jokes?"

Rafe shrugged. "I like her for you. Love is a rare and wonderful thing. Few find it, and even fewer manage to keep it. I hope your union is blessed."

All of us around the table gaped at him.

"Did he bump his head?" Matthias muttered.

"Maybe they finally replaced him with a robot," Dylan whispered from somewhere behind me.

Even Noah looked like he wasn't sure what to make of his brother-in-law's sudden good wishes. And they had been best friends since Lucia was a kid.

If Noah was the strong and silent type, Rafe was the invisible and deadly type. Seriously I don't think the guy had said this many words to me before. Ever. Usually he just glared at me with menace in his eyes until I backed down and left him alone.

Now I felt like shit for giving him such a hard time over the years.

"Thank you."

Suddenly Rafe's lips twitched. "Besides, I have a feeling Hailey is going to kick you in the ball and chain often enough that I won't have to."

The room erupted into laughter and good-natured jeers.

"There it is! Was worried about you for a minute there, mate." Matthias gave him a mock salute.

"*Annnnnnd* he's back," Dylan drawled.

I pressed my hand to my heart. "Coming from you, Rafe, that's better than a Hallmark card. I'll take it." I glanced over at Noah. "How did you know? Lucia?"

He nodded. "You realize what you've started right?"

"What? I just proposed last night, how could I have messed up already? It's not a big deal, we're just going to do something small."

"Something you'll remember this time?" Rafe asked innocently.

I put both of my middle fingers up and stood. "Fuck this. I'm going to find my bride. She'll be nice to me."

Noah looked like he was trying to cover a smile. "Okay but don't say I didn't warn you."

Ignoring all of them, I escaped the conference room while I still could. Hailey had some work with her that she'd planned to complete over the weekend, but we were both determined to carve out more time to spend together. Maybe I'd take her out to look for a dress later. It shouldn't be that hard to find a wedding dress in the greatest city on earth, right? I might not have been born a New Yorker, but I had as much passion and zeal for my adopted hometown as anyone born there.

"Hailey, did you want... What the hell happened?"

I skirted around the racks of clothes in the hallway that were blocking the entrance to the kitchen. "Hailey!"

"In here!"

I walked toward the sound of her voice and paused at the entrance to the family room. Every possible surface was covered with flowers, lace or fabric. An extremely sexy negligee was laid across the back of the couch next to JJ, who was talking a mile a minute into her phone. On the other side of the room, Lucia scribbled furiously on a clipboard while listening to Gemma. Diana stood right behind her, one hand on her pregnant belly looking like a general waiting to go into battle.

"Where is my wife?" I finally asked, exasperated.

JJ pointed to the center of the room vaguely. I peered closer. There was a bundle of fabric that finally shifted and turned.

"Holy shit. Butterfly, you look like you've been attacked by a disgruntled evening gown."

Hailey bit her lip, and I could see by the look in her eyes that she was trying not to laugh. "It turns out your friends take wedding planning really seriously. They called all their friends in fashion who then delivered all this stuff. I'm supposed to be trying on dresses, but I lost hope after this one. Plus, I think I'm stuck."

I tugged at the top of the dress, giving up when I heard something rip. "Oops, okay so that didn't work."

Hailey had tears in her eyes at that point from laughing so hard. "I really hope this isn't a bad omen."

"No way. If anything, this is a sign that asking the terrible twosome over there to help with the wedding was a bad idea."

JJ stepped between us. "Oskar, you guys need to pick up flowers and tuxedos. I found a shop that can rent them immediately, and we already had all of your measurements from Lucia's wedding. Hope you haven't gained weight!"

From behind her, Hailey mouthed, *Help me!*

I smothered a laugh. Normally I would love to be her knight in shining armor, but there was a really important errand that couldn't wait any longer. JJ had just given me the perfect excuse to leave without raising any suspicion.

"Flowers and tuxes. Right. We'll get on that." I leaned past her to kiss Hailey on the forehead. "Hang in there."

CHAPTER NINETEEN

Oskar

"Noah, do you mind if you guys head out and get your tuxes? Can you pick mine up too? There's an errand I want to run."

Noah lifted a brow. "Where are you going?"

I tried to hide my smile, but I couldn't. "Well, when we got married the first time, I didn't exactly have the kind of ring that I wanted to give her. So, I'm going to go to the jeweler and pick it up. I already called. It's ready now, so..."

Noah clapped me on the back. "Got to say, it's nice seeing you put down some roots."

"What do you mean?"

"Oh, come on, do you think I didn't notice that while you've been here, a part of you always had one foot out the door?"

I shifted on my feet. "Ah, been that apparent, huh?"

"Yeah," he shrugged. "I mean, I can tell you guys that we are family, but ultimately you guys decide. You have to choose whether you're here for good or going to up and bounce one day. So, I'm glad you decided."

"Yeah well, once you went to bat for me it wasn't like I was ever going to leave. You basically saved my life. I believe in repaying debts."

He shrugged. "Yeah well, that too."

We engaged in an awkward bro-hug scenario, and then he headed out with the rest of the waiting crew to get their tuxes fitted. Matthias and Jonas both gave me a questioning look before heading off with Noah, but I gave them a brief nod letting them know I'd be right there.

Rafe, surprisingly, didn't seem at all concerned I wasn't going with them to get my tux fitted. But then that motherfucker knew everything, so he probably knew what I was up to, already. Which was annoying, to say the least.

I popped into the jewelry store with a smile on my face. Helmer Monat was one of the best jewelers in the city. We'd helped him out with a spot of trouble a few years back when a family heirloom went missing. It had been in his family since, well, for centuries. When we'd helped him recover it, he said he owed us a favor, so I'd called mine in.

"Mr. Mueller, I was very excited to create this ring for you."

I grinned. "Yeah, I'm really excited to give it to her. I'm sort of doing this the backward way since we're already married. This time I'm doing it the right way."

"This is a special ring."

"Well, this is special woman."

He presented me with a jewelry box. When I opened it, encased in velvet was a ring in the shape of a butterfly. Maybe it was a little cheesy, but we were both kind of cheesy, and I hoped she would love it.

I left the jeweler's and checked the to-do list. I tried to

finish off two more items on the list. JJ would be happier, which meant she'd get off our case.

And I could have one last night with all the guys. This would be one hell of a bachelor party. I hoped. I mean, they should at least have planned for strippers.

Like you want strippers when you have the real thing at home.

Yeah, not really my thing. When the hell had that happened? I was a guy. I could pretty much always go for naked women.

But the moment I'd found Hailey again, it had been all Hailey all the time. I honestly couldn't think about a moment without her.

You've got it bad.

Yes. Yes, I did.

I hopped in the car just as my phone chimed, just one beep, and then three seconds later another beep. *Oh shit.* Frantically, I called the penthouse. I tried to get a hold of Tyse, but instead it was Gemma who answered. "Blake Security."

"Gemma, I just got a distress signal from Matthias."

"Shit, where are you guys?"

"I sent them to get the tuxes, while I picked up something for Hailey, so I'm about ten blocks away at Helmer's Jewelers."

"Okay, we'll meet you there."

Her? Matthias would kill me. "No, send Tyse."

"And I told you, we're on our way." She hung up without much preamble, and I honestly didn't have time to argue. My team was in trouble. And I needed to get there fast.

***

Hailey

"What was that?"

Gemma's lips were pressed into a thin line. "That was Oskar. They have trouble. We've got to go."

The bottom fell out of my stomach. "I'm going too."

Gemma looked like she wanted to tell me I couldn't, but then she asked me, "Can you shoot?"

"Yes. It was part of the anti-kidnap training my father sent us on. I was sixteen or somewhere around that age, I think. It's been a while, but I do know how to take a safety off."

"Fine. Come here. Diana, JJ, Lucia, let's go."

I trailed her as the rest of the women throughout the penthouse followed the sound of her voice into the weapons room. Tyse and Dylan were quick on our heels.

"What the hell do you think you're doing?" Tyse's voice was terse. And he looked none too pleased with Gemma as she opened up a drawer full of handguns. "What I'm doing is going to save my man. We got a distress call. Matthias and the others are pinned down at Han's Tuxedo, the tailor. Oskar is on his way."

I breathed deep. "Oskar wasn't with them?"

She shook her head. "He had another errand. He's only got one weapon. I don't know how armed the other guys are."

"Okay, give me a gun."

Gemma smirked and handed me a small handgun. But when I checked the clip, made sure the safety worked, weighed it in my hand, then pointed it at the bull's eye, she stepped back and gave me a little nod of appreciation. "Okay then, you were serious about having fired before."

"Yeah. My father was really serious about safety. I'm not sure why, but whatever."

JJ shrugged. "Well, as for me, I always have my piece on." She opened her purse and pulled out a sparkly gun.

Lucia snorted. "You bedazzled your gun? What the hell?"

JJ grinned. "I gave it some pizzazz. Just because I'm carrying doesn't mean I can't be stylish."

Diana just chuckled. Gemma rolled her eyes but laughed quietly. From the door, Tyse was shaking his head. "There is no way. You guys are going to have to go through me if you think you're getting out of here."

Gemma strapped guns to her body and a couple of knives. Then she turned to face Tyse with a smile. "Now Tyse, you really don't want me to have to go through you. The others, they'll play nice. But don't forget, I'm also ORUS."

His gaze narrowed then, and he crossed his arms. "And I

was ORUS, so we can do this all day. But you're not getting past me."

"Are you sure about that?" She strapped more knives to her, and he frowned. She grinned. "And do I have to remind you who my fiancé is? You have heard the stories, right? I fought Matthias and lived to tell the tale."

Tyse swallowed hard. I still didn't know what the deal was with Matthias. The guy seemed perfectly nice to me. A little intense maybe, but was he some extra level of badass? I'd make it a point to ask Oskar later.

"Gemma, don't do this. I don't want to fight with you. I certainly don't want to fight with Matthias later. But they're going to fire me if I let you guys go."

"Think of it like this, you can go down there and do what you can, but they're going to need more than one set of hands, right? So, you might as well stay here and provide extra protection for the Lucia and the kids, and let me, Diana, JJ, and Hailey go."

He shifted on his feet as he glanced around all of us carrying weapons. Gemma, obviously, was the most comfortable, Diana after her. JJ slammed her cross body on, like she was going on a shopping trip, but something about her gaze and the determination in her eyes told me she knew exactly what she was doing. And then there was me, with nowhere to put my gun. JJ gave me a smile, opened a bottom drawer, and pulled out a cross body. "Here you go. This will hold your gun, your keys, your wallet too, and plenty of room for lipstick."

I nodded my thanks and then slipped the bag on. I was officially a badass. *Hardly*, but close.

Tyse rolled his eyes. "Okay, but I'm coming with you guys."

She shook her head. "I don't know what we're facing. If it's an attack on Blake Security, you and Dylan are the last lines of defense For Lucia and Izzy. Well technically, Lucia is the last line."

Lucia grinned and hopped down from the counter. "Yup, I'm strapped with knives." She opened the cardigan she was wearing, and sure enough, she had some kind of belt thing with knives. What the hell was she going to do with knives?

"If anyone comes for the baby, I'll be in the panic room, and I've got them."

Tyse shuddered. JJ grinned appreciatively at her best

friend. "Yeah, Matthias has been training her. It turns out Lucia is kind of a badass with those knives."

Lucia agreed. "Yup, but it's better to have two body guards with guns. I'm not great with guns. But knives, I can do."

Tyse groaned. "You know those are close combat."

"Let me be clear, if anyone makes it through you and Dylan, it's going to be close combat. No one's touching my baby."

He sighed. And the moment he did, we knew we were golden.

In a matter of minutes, we were down in the car and flying like a bat out of hell. JJ drove like an insane person. Like a drunken insane person wearing a blindfold. But when we arrived in the alley two blocks over from the tailor, she drove in and parked with a screech. "Everybody out."

I inhaled deeply. Oskar had been saving me for weeks. It was time I help save him.

CHAPTER TWENTY

Oskar

I made my way around the back of the tuxedo shop. Most of the exterior was concrete, but there was one large bay window. A quick peek around a pillar told me someone had my whole crew tied with zip ties. Mother. Fucker.

The real hell came when another furtive look told me exactly who it was. An unholy blast from my past.

Fucking Mr. X. I'd thought I was rid of that guy once and for all. For years, I'd been walking around free and clear. I hadn't had to pay for any of my past sins. I'd been able to leave the organization unscathed. Mr. X had gone to prison, and I was a free man. All thanks to Noah.

I would have even been allowed to go back to my old life if I'd wanted. But Noah and the rest of the guys had given me more reason to stay. A home. A real family. A purpose. No way was I letting this happen.

I did the one thing I knew Noah would kill me for. I made a decision I might not be able to walk away from, but one I could be proud of.

I stepped out from the shadows and called out my past. "Mr. X, buddy, come on man, now you're just being extra as fuck. If you wanted to talk, all you had to do was call."

The voice that responded was loud, booming, and all too familiar. "Mueller. You're back. I was wondering where you'd run to. Our men had their eyes on you, but then you split with the team. I thought, that's my boy, always looking out for himself. But looks like even you are capable of surprises. You want to come out? Play with your friends?"

I wasn't dumb. I stayed behind the pillar. That's what training told me to do. But I had no intention of staying there for long. I'd happily sacrifice myself for the men who'd saved my ass dozens of times. But I'd take some bodies with me first.

One more look and I could see Mathias trying to work his hands in the zip ties. The problem was he had no leverage to break them. If he did, it would be a real fucking problem for Mr. X.

Noah was the same. As was Rafe. Jonas at least had a shot. He was closest to the wall, and there was some kind of... something sticking out of the wall. If it was at all rough, he might be able to get one of the zip ties off.

"Mr. X, let's talk about this man. Like I said, I'm open to anything. This seems a little extreme just to have a conversation."

"Well, because you declined to work for me, I lost a lot of money. I don't like losing money."

"I hear you. You lost a little cheddar. But that's hardly my fault. I know you think I should have just taken the job with you. And you know what, there's a part of me that maybe thinks I should have just taken the job too. But, as you lost two of your previous accountants to 'unfortunate circumstances,' you can see how it wasn't really in my best interest to come work for you. Once I saw my way out, I had to decline your generous offer of employment."

Yeah, motherfucker, because working for a psycho wasn't high in my list of priorities. And, yes, I might have gotten half his team killed. "Let me come in. You and I can talk. You can string me up from my toes, it will be great. But you gotta let my boys go."

Mr. X laughed then. "Because of you not showing up for that client meeting in Vegas, I lost three good men. Because of you not agreeing to watch my money, I used substandard help. So really, my men dying on that day in Vegas... that was your fault. I lost my brother."

Wow, the guy was a true narcissist. It wasn't my fault that the Feds had been called on Mr. X. Actually, it kind of was since I'd been the one to call them. But that was beside the point, and I wasn't telling him that. "Listen, I get it. You had some kind of shootout with the Feds. Blame me. Fine. Blame me. These guys, especially the kid, he had nothing to do with that. The British one, he's just an errand boy."

. . .

"Oh yeah? Something tells me I shouldn't believe you."

"Ah, well, it's up to you. The other one, the clean cut one, he's just a kid himself. Let one of them go to show some good faith, and I'll come in and we can talk about this like adults."

"You mean Lieutenant First Class Ryan Delaney? Former SEAL?"

Fuck, why the fuck did he know who the hell we were? Delaney had come from a clean background, so he'd gotten to keep his real last name. Dylan too. I'd taken my mother's maiden name. I'd never been arrested for anything, but my real last name could have been problematic. Everyone else who he would have looked up, he wouldn't have found military records on. And he shouldn't have found Delaney either. Unless he talked to someone that Delaney knew, which meant he'd been watching me for a while. A long while.

"Okay, fine. Maybe he was a Lieutenant, but mostly people push them around, honestly. Look at the kid. He's scrawny."

Compared to me, Noah, and Rafe, he was scrawny. He

was leaner, like Matthias. But I happen to personally know he's a crack shot.

Finally, the lock gave way, and I started to turn the door knob. "Listen, I'm coming in. I just want to talk. I'm tossing you my weapon."

Mr. X wasn't fucking around. Just because I could see him didn't mean he didn't have backup.

When I stepped in, I saw his backup. He had four guards. And then I noticed there were little packs under the chairs. Ah, explosives, fucking fabulous. "Okay, I'm here. You got me. Let's get this show on the road, shall we?" Today was not a good day to die, so I really fucking hoped Gemma, Diana, and Tyse were on their way. I just prayed I could stall this asshole until then.

Hailey

"Okay, how does this work?" I'd never in my life had to be a badass. Were there classes for that or something?

As everyone piled out of the car, armed and strapped like

they were going to war, I watched in awe. Somehow, I didn't feel entirely useful with just my baby gun.

Gemma checked her phone again. "I am so glad that man keeps his GPS tracker on just for me."

I frowned.

"Is that wise? What if people are trying to find us?"

She smiled.

"It's not just any GPS tracker. This is behind a million firewalls in a completely unfindable place. But it gives me the ultimate homing beacon on my man."

JJ snorted. "God help that man if he ever fucks up because we're all going to hunt him down and kill him."

"Why does every conversation that we have with you end up in someone getting maimed?" Diana asked with a chuckle.

JJ shrugged. "That's just me. Love me or hate me."

I laughed. "I think we'll all choose to love you."

She grinned. "Yup, that's the safest bet."

Gemma pointed at the roof. "I'm going up there. Hopefully I can get a clean shot."

Diana nodded. "Good, I'm going to have a quick look inside and see what we're working with." She turned to me. "Hailey, you come with me, okay?"

I slid a glance over at JJ. "What are you going to do?"

She grinned and gave me a wink. "I'm going to do what I do best. Distraction."

When JJ and Gemma headed off to their posts, I followed behind Diana, not sure of how this was going to work. I worried about her for starters. She was barely showing, but she was pregnant. Could she do this?

Pregnant women had been doing hard things for millennia.

If she said she was fine, then I was fine. And truth be told, she was a big time badass. After all, she'd carried off a whole undercover thing on Rafe. I needed to respect that hustle.

We headed around the building, and then she held up her hand. I didn't know exactly what the signal meant, but she stopped, so I stopped.

She *tsked* as she shook her head. "Oh my God, they've all been caught. Every last one of them. You wouldn't know that they were a den of badasses and thieves."

"What do you see?" I asked.

"Well, they've got all the guys tied up to chairs. Let me work this scope. One sec. The scope will allow us to get a better look."

Through the visor she got a good lay of the land. "Okay we have five assholes. And more bad news... the boys are sitting on explosives."

"That sounds like a recipe for disaster. No way we can go in guns blazing."

Diana shook her head. "Uh, no. We are not going to do that. We are going to wait."

I frowned. "For what?" Then I heard it, the commotion. Inside. Men shouting, fast talking. "Is that—"

Diana turned to me and grinned. "Yup. That's JJ. That is our distraction."

I strained to listen.

"Oh my God, I need to speak to someone in charge. I brought my leather jacket in for cleaning, and you messed it up."

One of the guards was trying to get her out of there. "Ma'am—"

That seemed to set JJ off. "Ma'am? I'm in my mid-20s. What the hell? Does this look like the body of a ma'am to you?" She kept going on and on. Yammering and muttering. Finally, another one of the guys went out front to help deal with her.

Diana held up two fingers. That meant we only had three guys left to deal with.

"Okay, so what do we do?"

"We wait for one more to go out and see what the hell the commotion is, and then we go in." She ducked down behind the back door, pulled out a black folded thing. It looked like some kind of tool kit.

"What is that?"

She grinned. "Lock pick set. We'll get you one of these, don't worry."

I blinked. "Am I sure I want one?"

"It's a girl's best friend."

In my ear com, Gemma laughed. "That and explosives.

I shook my head. "You guys are just as badass as the guys."

Diana grinned. "More so. And you can tell them that too."

Inside, JJ was yelling and cussing. One of them threatened to carry her out.

"If you put a hand on me, I swear to God I will take my shoe off and beat you with it."

I peered around the window again briefly. I could see Oskar. He looked furious, tense, tight. Like he was waiting for something.

"How are going to do this?" I asked.

"The last guy in there will be the one with the detonator. He won't chance going in the other room with it in case JJ's a trap. So that's the guy we need to take out before he blows our guys sky high."

I blinked at how she said it... like it was a real possibility.

"Okay wait for it. You're going to get the signal. Then we're going to go in."

"What's the signal?" I asked.

Suddenly I heard JJ screech at the top of her lungs. "I've already called the police. I'll have you all arrested for leathertricide. Leather death."

One of the guys shouted. "What the hell? Did she say cops?"

Diana chuckled. "That's our go-sign."

Next thing I knew, we had our guns out and were moving quickly. Diana had the door open, and then shots were fired. She bolted forward, launching herself at the idiot with the detonator. It went flying and we all held our breath. When it didn't go off, the fight was on.

He was big, but she hung on valiantly. I ran up behind him and did the one thing I could think of... I kicked him in the nuts. He fell to his knees, and Diana elbowed him in the face. He sagged and passed out.

Diana cursed as she gingerly picked the detonator up off the ground.

The other men came running in. Suddenly, there was a crack of gunfire and glass breaking, and the first guy fell to his knees, a bright red hole in his forehead. The next one came in, and Diana rolled over, aimed her gun, and shot him too.

There was another man in a suit with his knife to Oskar's throat, and I didn't even think about it. I raised my gun. Aimed it. Fired. It was a wonder I didn't hit Oskar. The guy with the knife clutched his shoulder, and then there was another crack just before a hole appeared in his temple. I heard a clicking sound, then JJ walked through the door with the last guy in front of her, and it looked like she had a gun to his back.

"If I were you, I'd stay perfectly still. We have snipers on the roof across the street. You want a hole in your head too?"

The guy shook his head.

Diana started to undo Rafe's ties, muttering the whole time about foolish men and the trouble they got themselves into.

I ran for Oskar.

His gaze on me was intense, heated. "Hey, butterfly. How you doing?"

I shook my head.

My hands were shaking, the blood rushing through my head. He was safe. He was safe.

He was okay.

"It's okay, baby. Listen there's a knife strapped to my ankle. Grab that, you can cut the ties."

I reached for his ankle and found the knife, shaking as I went to work. Noah was released next, and then Matthias was eased off of his chair by Diana and Rafe.

As soon as Oskar was released, his arms wound around me, tight, holding me to him. "Oh my God. What did you do?"

I grinned up at him. "Looks like we saved your asses."

He smoothed back my hair and blinked away tears. "That you did. I love you so much."

"Me too. But maybe you try not to get killed for at least another couple of years?"

"Yeah. I think we can manage that."

CHAPTER TWENTY-ONE

Oskar

I was beyond pissed.

Relieved, yes. All my mates were bloody alive and kicking, as Matthias would say, but that had been a close call.

As mad as I was though, Noah was on a different level.

We all walked through the doors of the Penthouse weary and exhausted, nerves frayed. Everyone filed into the living room and dropped their tuxedos across the couches. Lucia came out. The first thing she did was hand Izzy off to Rafe, and then she leapt into Noah's arms. "I swear to God, if you ever scare me like that again, I will kill you myself."

He held her tight, kissed her forehead and then set her down. When Tyse and Dylan came back in to join the rest of us, he glared at them. "Do you want to explain to me what the fuck happened and how the women ended up in the field?"

Tyse narrowed his gaze. I couldn't wait for this explanation. "With all due respect Noah, I think these women saved your asses. Gemma and Diana, as they've already shown, are more than capable. JJ, well, she's just terrifying. I have yet to see Hailey in the field, but if she's back alive..."

Tyse didn't flinch. I was going to kill the kid myself. I took a step toward him, and Matthias put a hand on my chest. I glared down at it until I saw who was on the other end of the appendage.

Matthias shook his head. "Nah, mate. You don't want any of that. And he's right. There's no one else I'd rather have come and get me. Gemma knows what she's doing. And, no offense, but she's prettier than you lot."

Gemma just laughed and shoved her way past him. "Ah, prettier *and* I've kicked your ass before."

He scowled. "I wouldn't say 'kicked my ass' exactly."

"Yeah, I hurt you. Everyone here knows it. You might as well admit it to yourself."

I scowled, but I pulled Hailey to me, and she snuggled right in. If Noah was going to yell, I didn't want him yelling at her.

Noah sighed. "Tyse, the job was to keep the women here. Not let them in the field."

Tyse crossed his arms. He seemed to have no problem standing up to us. "No, there was no job. Yes, basic security of the penthouse. If anything comes in, kill it. We would have managed that. And not for nothing, Lucia looks pretty insane with those knives strapped to her, so I'm sure she would have liked to help out. You're doing them a disservice by saying the women can't do anything. You were supposed to go and get your tuxedos and some flowers, but instead you got yourselves nicked, so decisions had to be made. Gemma answered the call, and you know full well she's just as capable as I am. Would you have rather Gemma and I wasted time fighting each other over who got the privilege to come bail your asses out? Isabella is the only person here who can't actually fight. She is the only one who needed protection, which is what I was doing with Dylan and Lucia."

Noah couldn't really argue. His mouth fell open. Diana stepped to the living room as well. She picked up Izzy and gave her niece a little kiss and then handed the baby to Noah. "There's a good girl. Your daddy is a moron, but you're a good girl."

Lucia snorted a laugh.

Diana continued. "I'll have you know that I'm the one who dug out the detonator so that JJ and Gemma and Hailey could rescue your sorry behinds. P.S. I'm also pregnant, so that makes me extra badass. And if you ever suggest that I am a little woman who needs to be rescued again, I will gut you and put your hearts on top of ice-cream, which right about now sounds really appetizing. Go ahead, you can say it now. You're grateful we were there."

Noah's mouth worked a few seconds, but somehow he finally managed to form the words. "Yes, we were grateful you were there, because we would have been in a mess if you weren't. Without you guys, we'd have been stuck."

JJ sauntered in. "Without *my* stellar acting skills, you'd still be stuck is what you mean."

Jonas just rolled his eyes. "Yes, baby, I think they heard you all over Manhattan."

"I should hope so. Someone needs to give me an Oscar. But I'm disappointed. I didn't even get to use my gun on more than one person."

Jonas turned to glare at Matthias. "See, this is what happens when I let you teach her how to shoot."

Matthias grinned. "She's a great shot, isn't she?"

"Yeah. But now she has a thirst for it, thanks to you," muttered Jonas.

Matthias only shrugged.

We heard a low-toned ring signaling someone was coming up. Rafe nodded at Noah and took off toward the foyer. I looked at Noah askance.

Noah confirmed what I suspected. "That's ORUS come to collect Mr. X's crew. They have a whole bunch of questions they want to ask them."

Something told me those assholes weren't headed to

central lock up. Nope, they were headed somewhere dark, dingy, and scary as fuck. But they'd tried to kill my brothers, so I didn't give a shit about where they'd end up.

Hailey snuggled in closer and I held her tighter, kissing the top of her head. "Are you okay?"

She nodded against my chest. "To be honest, I'm not really sure."

"Well, the good news is I don't think you killed him. We've got three live ones. Ryan's bringing them up now."

"He's still alive?"

"Yeah, he's still alive. They were all wearing vests. But you were fucking amazing. When you shot him, you hit him straight in the chest. He passed out. The shot you got off, that's what downed him."

"Thank God."

"I'm really proud of you, and I cannot wait to marry you."

"Can you just go ahead and promise me that the rest of our marriage will not be quite so entertaining?"

I really wished I could. "Yeah, about that. Sometimes, things get a little crazy around here. Okay, a lot of times. I'm not going to lie. But we're a team. Better than that, we're a family."

Noah was still glaring at Tyse. And Tyse was not backing down. I liked the kid already.

"Fine, it was the right call," Noah finally muttered. "Gemma, Diana, JJ, and Hailey, thank you for saving our bacon."

Hailey turned around and grinned. "You're very welcome. Now if you guys don't mind, I'd like to get some rest so I can get married tomorrow."

Noah nodded. "Yeah, I think we could all use some rest." Isabella slapped her father in the face and shook her head. She used her chubby little fingers to make sign language for 'no bed time.'

I laughed. Only Izzy would say no bedtime after an ordeal like today. In that moment, all I wanted to do was get into bed and hold my wife close. Tomorrow, I would get to remember marrying her.

Hailey

We were really doing it, after everything we'd been through. After losing Oskar once, and then nearly losing him again, I planned to keep this man forever and I couldn't wait.

"You look like the cat that swallowed the canary."

I pinned the wedding corsage on his tux. "You recognize no one should look this good in a tuxedo, right?

He grinned, his blue eyes full of warmth and love. "I can't help it. I make most things look good."

I just shook my head and laughed. "Of course you would say that."

"Of course I would. Being outrageous is part of my charm."

"Are you sure you want to do this? There's no backing out now. You can't claim you don't remember."

He took my hands and clasped them in his gigantic ones. "From the moment I found out we'd gotten married in Las Vegas, I knew I was keeping you. I just wanted to give you time to come around to my way of thinking."

I shook my head. "You did not know."

"Maybe not consciously, but I definitely felt it. I didn't want to let you go. Just the idea of it pissed me off. And now we get to make it official with our friends and family. For the first time in my life, I want to put down roots. I want to do this. I'm just so glad you're back in my life, and I am never letting you go."

"Someone has been practicing their vows."

"Pretty much every day since you walked back into my life."

I swallowed back tears. "You realize you're going to make me cry, right?"

"No, no tears today. I think you've had enough tears. Today, my wife only gets to be happy."

I grinned at that. "God, I'm really going to get used to that."

"Yeah, me too. I'm especially going to get used to all the awesome parts of being close to you."

He leaned forward and nuzzled my neck, kissing along my jaw. "Are you sure you want to go out there? I say we take our time. They can wait. They're not going to start without us."

I slapped his shoulder. "We're getting married. I'm not going to wait to make it official, official. I can't wait to be Mrs. Oskar Mueller."

He grinned. "Is this a bad time to tell you that my last name is not Mueller?"

I stared at him. "What?"

"It's actually Schilling, but when we all joined Blake Security, those of us with shady reputations changed our names and took new identities. Mueller is actually my mother's maiden name."

I blinked. "Oh my God, you know what? I'm going to take Mueller, because that's your current *legal* name, right?"

"You don't have to add a question mark to that. That's my legal name. That's who I am now. Oscar Schilling doesn't exist anymore. The man who I was doesn't exist. The man you see in front of you lives to make you happy. That's all."

"Well in that case, that's the guy I want to marry."

"Then let's do this. I love you. I always have."

"Right back at you." I took his hands and squeezed. For once, I wasn't at all terrified to let go.

CHAPTER TWENTY-TWO

Oskar

I tugged nervously at my collar again. It wasn't too tight, but it still felt like it was strangling me.

"Tell me I'm crazy for agreeing to this."

"You're crazy," Jonas replied. "Dude, you're already married. You had the best excuse ever for actually skipping this bullshit."

He glanced over his shoulder nervously and then relaxed.

"Don't let your wife hear you say that." I had to give the guy credit. He was married to JJ and dealt with her every day. I couldn't even tease him about looking over his shoulder.

"Stop fidgeting. She's not going to leave you. If she's spent this much time with you and hasn't bailed yet, I'd say you have her well and truly fooled."

I glanced over at Rafe. "Just admit it. You love me. Secretly, deep down somewhere in that black heart of yours."

He chuckled. "You wish, jackass. But I am happy that Hailey has someone to protect her the way she deserves. She's one of the good ones."

Jonas appeared at my elbow holding a small highball of scotch. "Drink this. You look like you're about to have a panic attack."

It was just Jonas and Rafe with me. Noah had gone to check if the women needed anything. We were in one of the guest rooms since Hailey was changing into her dress in our room. God, who had come up with the asinine idea to make a man wait for his bride in a separate area? If I didn't think Rafe would tackle me, I would charge out there and go find my bride. But considering that JJ had given us orders to wait here until it was time, I wasn't willing to risk it.

No one wanted to deal with a pissed-off Jessica Jones, least of all me.

The door opened and we all looked up as Noah walked back in. "They're almost ready. Hailey's parents are here, by the way."

My shoulders sagged in relief. In the wake of everything we'd discovered about her brother, Hailey hadn't been sure her parents would even show up if we invited them. But in the end, she'd decided to take the high road. As she put it, "They're my parents, and I want to do the right thing even if they don't."

"Good. That'll make Hailey happy. She deserves that much."

I couldn't give her a normal life. It wasn't like I had a normal set of parents to introduce her to since my mom was gone and my father and I mutually ignored each other. But if I could help her preserve her relationship with her parents, I would. As for her brother, Evan could fuck off. Hailey was still heartbroken after learning the truth about what he'd done in the past, but if I knew my softhearted wife, she'd eventually forgive him.

So I needed to start working on my tolerant face now.

Currently it looked like a cross between road rage and constipation.

"Happy wife, happy life," Noah muttered. "This is some A-level advice I'm giving you here."

I shook my head. It felt good to have us all there. In a way it felt like the end of an era. All of us had started together in various stages of our lives, but we were all dealing with ghosts from the past. Now here we were, all married and on the other side. Proof that even bad guys could get a happy ending if they worked hard enough for it.

That was the secret, I guessed. You had to actually work for it. And be worthy of it. Which was an ongoing process.

"I want to say something before the others get here."

Rafe, Jonas and Noah all stared back at me with knowing eyes. And I realized they'd already given me the best gift, knowing that they'd have my back no matter what, no questions asked. I didn't need to pull some long speech out of my ass to thank them, either. They already knew.

"I'm still the prettiest."

Moving quickly, I ducked out of the way as Jonas tossed the paper program at my head. I caught it in mid-air.

"How the hell did JJ get a program printed that fast?"

He shrugged. "She knew some guy at the printer. I didn't ask any questions. Not sure I want to know."

The program featured a gorgeous picture of Hailey and a picture of me in the middle of eating a hot dog.

"I see your wife takes her revenge at the best moments."

He chuckled. "No one plays the long game like that woman."

The door opened, and JJ appeared as if she'd been summoned. "We're almost ready to start. Oskar, the bride has requested to see you. You'll stay outside the door because she wants her dress to be a surprise."

I jumped at the chance to see Hailey before we had to stand in front of whatever minister Noah had scrounged up to perform the ceremony. "Okay."

JJ pinned me with a scary look. "And no hanky-panky. I did her makeup, and it's perfect."

I grinned, because me seeing Hailey and not messing up her makeup had a probability hovering somewhere around zero, but I was willing to say whatever was necessary if it got me there.

"You got it. Now, I need to see my wife."

Hailey

At the knock on the door, I rushed forward to open it. After being poked and prodded for the last hour, I needed to see Oskar. He was my reminder of why I'd willingly signed up to squeeze myself into a sample-sized dress and put on heels that I could barely walk in.

Not to mention the pound of makeup JJ had plastered to my face. I needed a break. And a reward.

When I pulled the door open, Oskar burst inside. Giggling, I shut it behind him quickly.

"What are you doing? I know JJ gave you the *don't look at her dress* speech."

"I don't care about that. I'm dying without you, and this tie is strangling me."

"Poor baby. You need a hug."

He came willingly, ducking his head so I could embrace

him. After a minute, one finger migrated to the bodice of my dress. I slapped it away.

"I was just checking that my beauties are still there. I'll see you later," he cooed in the direction of my cleavage.

"You are crazy."

"And you love me," he said, his eyes locked on mine.

"You know it. I love you, and I can't wait until we can be alone again. Why did we think a wedding was a good idea again?"

He swept me up into his arms and swung me around. "Hell if I know, but if you want me to bust us out, just say the word. I'm your hero, baby."

Laughing, I extricated myself from his arms and smoothed my dress. "Lucia and JJ worked so hard on this ceremony. We can't disappoint them. And my parents actually showed up, so we need to go out there and do this thing so our friends and family can be a part of our day."

"We're pretty lucky, huh?"

I knew what he meant. That the girls had worked so hard

to pull this together for us literally overnight was a testament to their love for us.

"Our friends are pretty great."

He laughed. "You know, when I met you that day three years ago, I could have never predicted this. I was alone in the world, trying to outrun the consequences of a lifetime of bad decisions and unsure of what the future held. Honestly at that point, I didn't really think I had a future. I always figured I'd bite it at the hands of one of my dad's enemies."

I pulled him down for a quick kiss. "The universe works in mysterious ways, huh? Now we're married, and we get to spend the rest of forever doing this."

There was a quick knock at the door before it opened slightly. "Are you messing up her makeup, He-Man?"

Oskar didn't bother to move back. "Yes. And enjoying it thoroughly."

"Good. I expected nothing less. Now get presentable. It's show time."

I glanced over at the full-length mirror, straightened the bodice of my dress, and wiped away a smudge of lipstick below my bottom lip.

When I turned around, Oskar was watching me with amusement. He held out an arm for me to take.

"Let's go do this thing."

And I followed my husband out of the room and toward a future that was still being written.

Thank you for reading STILL BRAZEN!

Several of the side characters in this duet are from our other books. Find out more about Sebastian, the Prince of the Winston Isles and Mya Taylor, the marketing agent with the funny story!

I never wanted the **throne**...

I have a plan: find my **long-lost brother** & make him the prince so I don't have to rule.

The last thing I have time for is my **sexy new neighbor**. She's everything I don't want, sassy, funny and...*not* available.

That's okay—I'm amazing best-guy-friend material.. **Friends? Sure.** Anything more? Definitely not.

All I have to do is **not touch her, kiss her or fanta-size about**...never mind...

It's not like I have a choice. I can't let her find out who I really am. And she's got secrets of her own.

Start Reading Cheeky Royal at
nanamaloneromance.net/cheekyroyal

My cock a doodle doo is on strike.

Yeah I know, I can't believe it either. Years of perfect performance and now this traitor decides to get picky. And the only woman who gets him going is my co-worker. Rival, she-devil and my competition for the biggest ad account this side of the Atlantic.

If we want to win the hottest wedding designer in the world, we have to prove we understand his business. Love. Passion. Marriage. But it turns out Mya isn't familiar with any of the above.

When I find out she's never taken a trip to O-town, we make a little wager. Not only will I win the client, but I'll prove to her that multiple O's are not a myth.

Start Reading Beg Me at mmalonebooks.com/begme

My best friend is happily coupled up and all he asked me to do is help keep her and her friend safe. But JJ is loud, argumentative and has more sass than sense. And to protect her I might have to break the vow I made years ago.

Book 1 of The Force Duet.

One-click the next book, Force!

She wanted to give him a heart attack.

As Jonas raced through the streets, his eyes went back to his phone again and again to follow the tracker Matthias had sent. A blinking red dot that represented the one woman who could crawl under his skin.

He turned at the next street and gunned the engine. Luckily he'd been close, so the crazy woman hadn't been walking alone for too long. She was determined to send them all into heart failure. What the hell was she thinking walking home this late by herself?

An open parking space ahead beckoned and Jonas almost took out a part of the curb as he swung into it. He jumped out and slammed the door behind him, locking the vehicle with his key fob. He'd deliberately aimed for a street ahead of her so he could intercept her. Not that she'd appreciate his forethought at all. No. He fully expected to get an earful and a sassy string of expletives from the always delightful Jessica Jones.

He didn't have to wait long. She was about ten feet away and still hadn't noticed him, another thing he'd be sure to spank her ass for later. Hadn't he taught her the importance of being aware of your surroundings? But JJ was in a world of her own, her hips swinging as she strode down the street. It was only as she got closer and he saw her face that he realized this wasn't just JJ flouting the rules for fun. Her eyes were wild and darted around her frantically. She was clutching her bag to her side, not so much like she was afraid someone would steal it, but like she just needed to hold on to something.

She wasn't breaking the rules. She was scared. Something had sent her running, and Jonas needed to know what it was.

Jonas didn't move so she almost crashed into him.

"Watch it, asshole!"

He grabbed her arm and they struggled for a moment. "JJ, calm down. It's me."

Her eyes locked onto him, and for a moment she looked so vulnerable that it broke his heart. "Baby girl, it's me. Matthias sent me your coordinates when he saw you leave work without an escort."

She nodded frantically then glanced behind her. "I had to go. I just needed to get out of there."

"Okay, well, we can go wherever you need to."

His words, meant to calm, seemed to enrage her. She pointed her finger at him, getting annoyingly close to his eyes.

"I know I can go where I need to. That's what I'm doing. I don't need a man to tell me where I can go. Nobody controls me!"

Jonas threw up his hands. "No one said you couldn't. I'm trying to help you. Do you know how reckless this was, walking out alone? Anything could have happened to you, crazy woman!"

JJ clutched her bag tighter. "I've walked home plenty of times by myself before."

"I don't think you need me to tell you that things are different now."

The words took the wind out of her sails. JJ sagged a little, her eyes meeting his directly.

"Yeah. I know."

He fell into step beside her, happy when she followed him back to where he'd parked the car. Their usual routine was for one of the guys to escort her home from the office. If she needed to stay late, like she had tonight, she would call them when she was ready to go and someone would pick her up. Ever since everything had gone down last year, when her best friend had been stalked, JJ had seemed to understand how serious this all was and had cooperated with their efforts to keep her protected.

What had happened tonight to change that? Jonas wasn't sure what was going on but there had to have been something to send her fleeing into the night looking as haunted as she had earlier.

He held the door open for her and waited as she climbed up into the vehicle. She settled her bag on her lap and then turned to grab the seatbelt. When she saw him still standing in the doorway to the car, she hesitated.

"Is everything okay?"

"Do I look okay to you?" When she recoiled at his harsh tone, Jonas took a deep breath. "Sorry. No. I'm not okay. Not at all."

Jonas didn't offer any other explanation, just shut the door and walked around to the driver's side. Let her stew on that. Maybe then she'd see what it felt like to be left out in the dark, wondering what the hell was going on.

Right before he reached the driver's side door, he stopped. He was angry. Not just annoyed or peeved, but truly angry. Because whatever had scared JJ badly enough to have her running out without a word to her security was something that she hadn't come to him about. That didn't feel right at all. As much as they bickered, did JJ really not know that he'd drop whatever he was doing to help her?

He took a deep breath before opening the door and getting behind the wheel. JJ looked over at him. What he was feeling must have been broadcast on his face because she groaned.

"I don't want to hear the lecture right now, okay? I was busy at work and just felt like going home without calling out the cavalry, okay?"

Jonas shook his head, unbelievably disappointed. Not just because she wasn't taking her own safety seriously but also at the boldfaced lie. Did she really think he was that unobservant? It was an insult to him, not just as a security agent but as a man. He saw everything about her. She loved Lucia like a sister and put up with her best friend's fussing, even though she hated to be hovered over. She liked to watch Oskar lifting weights, much to Jonas's annoyance and jealousy.

He knew that she had a serious love affair with vodka. She had a hate affair with men and always chose badly. Including the dipshits she dated who didn't even bother to pick her up at home.

So why would she think he wouldn't see through such an obvious lie?

"I'm not going to give you a lecture, JJ. Just a reminder. If shit goes bad, we can't help you if we don't know where you are."

Jonas had expected her to have a scathing response or to tell him where to stick it. But what JJ did next was the absolute last thing he'd ever expected. She turned to him with big blue eyes.

And burst into tears.

JJ had been only seven when she first discovered the power of tears.

She'd gotten caught by her father sneaking a cookie. Her dad was a stickler for the no-sweets-before-dinner rule. Sneaking a cookie without asking was grounds for losing her television privileges. The moment her eyes had filled with tears, her father had started to shift on his feet. She'd added a sniffle and before she knew it, he was shoving a cookie at her.

She'd learned it applied to men in general when she'd tried it on her first boyfriend at the age of twelve, Sal Morini. Sal had tried to break up with her before the seventh grade dance so he could go out with a girl who'd put out. Namely Vicki Dematto. As soon as she'd turned on the tears, he'd backtracked. Of course at the dance she'd ditched him to party with Lucia and her friends, then told Vicci Dematto what he'd said. No girl had gone out with Sal the rest of the year.

Those early experiences had been eye-opening experiences and led to an epiphany for JJ. Ever since, she'd never had an issue using her big blue eyes to get her out of trouble.

But this time, she wasn't pulling a sympathy card or being manipulative at all. She was honestly just overwhelmed.

And furious that Jonas was the one to witness it.

But, he didn't seem to be enjoying it any more than she was. He stared at her in shock before swinging his eyes back to the road.

"Oh God, I'm sorry. I wasn't trying to yell at you."

Hearing him backtracking somehow only made it worse. She was a strong, independent woman and she didn't need to be pandered to. It was humiliating that she was crying right now when all she wanted to do was rage, but after being so sure that someone was following her, her emotions were raw and right at the surface.

"I'm not crying about that. Damn it, why am I crying at all?" She swiped at her cheeks and glared at him, as if the tears were his fault.

Although maybe they were partially his fault. She'd been holding it together while walking on her own. Then Jonas had to show up looking all kinds of edible and reminding her how much her safety meant to everyone else. Of course she'd broken down! What woman wouldn't, after a guilt trip like that?

Never mind that what he'd said wasn't even that bad. JJ needed someone to blame just then, and Jonas was readily available.

"You show up talking about Lucia and my safety. I thought someone was following me, so I told him I had a Taser and a dick, but really, all I had was the dick and I was scared, because even if that dick is huge, I mean it's probably more effective as a club."

Jonas glanced at her from the corner of his eye, and then mouthed the word *dick* slowly. Under any other circumstances JJ would have laughed. He had the cautious expression you use when talking to someone who is completely batshit crazy.

Maybe she had lost it. She reached back into her purse and pulled it out. "See, I have a legitimate dick."

His eyes went wide. "Damn, I think that thing is setting some unrealistic expectations."

She rolled her eyes. "It's not for me to use, asshole. It was a gag gift that Lucia gave back. And it was all I had as a weapon."

He worked hard to wipe the smirk off his face. "Jessica, I apologize if I made you feel like I was coming down hard on you. I just want you to know that your safety is our top priority."

He made another turn that had her shifting slightly, almost falling into the door. Part of her wanted to give him shit for his driving, but she couldn't even muster the energy. She'd been running on pure adrenaline before, but now that she was tucked into the safe confines of the car with Jonas, the fear from before came back full force. What the hell had that been about? She'd heard something; there was no way she'd imagined that. And if she'd heard something, and someone had been there, why hadn't they answered when she called out? Why would anyone want to scare her?

She ignored the voice in the back of her head. *You know who might.*

No. That was her old life. Things were different now. *Are you sure? Because maybe the fire wasn't an accident.*

She couldn't go down that spiral again. She had a brand new life now.

They pulled into the underground garage in the Blake Security building. JJ had been so deep in her thoughts that she hadn't even realized they were home. *Home.* The place you were supposed to feel safe. JJ hadn't felt like that about any place in a long time. But she could honestly acknowledge that she'd felt like that the past few months living with Lucia and her crew. Her living arrangements had seemed like a gross overreaction to her friend's security issues the prior year, but she'd soon come to love it. Surrounded by muscular, hot men all the time and living rent free. Not a bad deal at all.

But now she could see that she'd allowed it to lull her into a false sense of security. Sure she was safer living with the Blake Security team, but she must never let herself think she was truly safe. No matter where she went, she would never be safe.

"You know you can come to me with anything, right?"

JJ looked over to see that Jonas had cut the car off and turned in his seat so he could watch her. Suddenly self-conscious, she pushed her hair behind her ear.

"Sure. I mean, it's your job."

"No. Not just because it's my job."

Awareness blossomed and JJ flushed. His eyes didn't leave hers. She fidgeted with the strap of her bag, unsure how to handle this side of him. It was weird to have him looking at her like this and being nice to her. Angry and argumentative Jonas? She could handle him with one hand tied behind her back. But tender, sex-on-a-stick Jonas? Well, she didn't have the first clue as to how to act. What if she admitted that she'd wanted to call him earlier? What if she told him that she thought of him when she was alone in her bed at night and he laughed?

She'd die instantly.

"Well, I'm fine," she protested weakly. "I don't need anyone's help."

"Maybe not, but I do."

"You need my help," JJ replied, deliberately misunderstanding him.

She could tell by the flare of heat in his eyes that he was gearing up for one of their knock down, drag out wars of words. Her body responded in kind. For the first time, she catalogued the symptoms like an outsider. Increased heart rate and breathing. Flushed skin and a sense of anticipation.

God. It was so obvious looking back on it now. The whole time they'd been fighting they'd been engaging in foreplay. She could only wonder if it was as obvious to everyone else in the house. Probably. Which was just great. How was she supposed to look the others in the eye now?

"I need you to want my help. I need to help you. Because the idea of anyone fucking with you makes me crazy."

The idea that Jonas would unleash his rage on someone just because they'd bothered her pleased her greatly. She clamped down on the response. It was far too close to a "girlfriend" type of thing, and way too possessive for her taste. She'd had more than enough of possessive men who thought they owned her.

"What did I just say? Something just made the light go out of your eyes."

She shook her head. "Nothing. But I don't want anyone getting hurt because of me. I just want to be left alone."

"Who isn't allowing you to be left alone?"

Damn him for being so smart. The only way to keep from giving him all the clues he needed was to distract him. Luckily, she knew the perfect way to do that.

"Right now the only one annoying me is you. So I guess I'll say thanks for the ride and good night."

Before he could react, she reached over the console and grabbed the front of his shirt. He let her tug him until he was close enough for her to smell the scent of his cologne. Their eyes met, and suddenly Jonas smiled. The impact of it, especially so close, made JJ feel like she was flying. And suddenly this wasn't about distracting him anymore. It was about doing what she'd wanted to do for ages.

Kiss him.

His lips softened under hers and he let out a soft groan that ricocheted through the still interior of the car. It was incredibly intimate, secluded there with just the two of them and the rapidly increasing sound of their breathing. For those moments, they weren't Jonas and JJ, mortal enemies.

They were two people who connected like lightning, taking each other in like they wanted to merge into one being.

She gasped and a moan slipped loose. Jonas took that opportunity to slip his hand into her hair, anchor her head, and deepen the kiss, his tongue sliding over hers expertly.

JJ hooked her arm around his neck, holding him still, and he opened his mouth wider like he was trying to swallow her whole. If the console hadn't been between them, she likely would have climbed into his lap, but instead she just sucked on his lower lip until he moaned into her mouth, the sound finally bringing her back to reality.

They stayed for a beat staring at each other before she pulled back and opened the door. The rush of cool air coming in cleared her head, and JJ wondered if it had finally happened. After years of pretending to be okay, if maybe she'd finally had a mental breakdown.

"JJ, what just—"

"Good night, Jonas." She closed the door and walked quickly to the elevator.

For the first time that day, luck was on her side, because after she leaned forward for the retinal scan, the doors opened immediately.

The doors closed just as Jonas rushed up. She heard his muffled curse get fainter as the elevator ascended.

"Good night, indeed." JJ touched her mouth.

One-click the next book, Force!

Also available at www.malonesquared.com/force

M. Malone is a *NYT & USA Today* Bestselling author of completely inappropriate romantic comedy. She spends most days wearing Wonder Woman leggings and T-shirts that she's embarrassed for anyone to see while she plays with her imaginary friends.

She lives with her husband and their two sons in the picturesque mountains of Northern Virginia even though she is afraid of insects, birds, butterflies and other humans. **minxmalone.com**

USA Today Bestselling Author, **NANA MALONE**'s love of all things romance and adventure started with a tattered romantic suspense she borrowed from her cousin on a sultry summer afternoon in Ghana at a precocious thirteen. She's been in love with kick butt heroines ever since.

With her overactive imagination, and channeling her inner Buffy, it was only a matter a time before she started creating her own characters. Waiting for her chance at a job as a ninja assassin, Nana, meantime works out her drama, passion and sass with fictional characters every bit as sassy and kick butt as she thinks she is. **nana-maloneromance.net**